Pan was founded in 1944 by Alan Bott, then owner of The Book Society. Over the next eight years he was joined by a consortium of four leading publishers – William Collins, Macmillan, Hodder & Stoughton and William Heinemann – and together they launched an imprint that is an international leader in popular paperback publishing to this day.

Pan's first mass-market paperback was *Ten Stories* by Rudyard Kipling. Published in 1947, and priced at one shilling and sixpence, it had a distinctive logo based on a design by artist and novelist Mervyn Peake. Paper was scarce in post-war Britain, but happily the Board of Trade agreed that Pan could print its books abroad and import them into Britain provided that they exported half the total number of books printed. The first batch of 250,000 books were dispatched from Paris to Pan's warehouse in Esher on an ex-Royal Navy launch named *Laloun*. The vessel's first mate, Gordon Young, was to become the first export manager for Pan.

Around fifty titles appeared in the first year, each with average print runs of 25,000 copies. Success came quickly, largely due to the choice of vibrant, descriptive

book covers that distinguished Pan books from the uniformity of Penguin paperbacks, which were the only real competitors at the time.

Pan's expertise lay in its ability to popularize its authors, and a combination of arresting design coupled with energetic marketing and sales helped turn the likes of Leslie Charteris, Eric Ambler, Nevil Shute, Ian Fleming and John Buchan into bestsellers. The first book to sell a million copies was *The Dam Busters* by Paul Brickhill, first published in 1951. Brickhill was among the first to receive a Golden Pan award, for sales of one million copies. His fellow prize winners in 1964 were Alan Sillitoe for *Saturday Night and Sunday Morning* and Ian Fleming, who won it seven times over. It was also given posthumously to Grace Metalious for *Peyton Place*.

In the Sixties and Seventies authors such as Dick Francis, Wilbur Smith and Jack Higgins joined the fold, and 1972 saw the founding of the ground-breaking literary paperback imprint, Picador. Then-Editorial Director Clarence Paget signed up the third novel by the relatively unknown John le Carré, and transformed the author's career. Pan also secured paperback rights in James Herriot's memoirs of a Yorkshire vet in 1973, and a year later fought off tough competition to publish *Jaws* by Peter Benchley. Inspector Morse made his first appearance in Colin Dexter's *Last Bus to Woodstock* in 1974.

By 1976 Pan had sold over 30 million copies of its books and was outperforming all its rivals. Over the ensuing decades they published some of the biggest names in popular fiction, such as Jackie Collins, Dick Francis, Martin Cruz Smith and Colin Forbes.

By the late Eighties, publishers had stopped buying and selling paperback licences and in 1987 Pan, now wholly owned by Macmillan, became its paperback imprint. This was a turbulent time of readjustment for Pan, but with characteristic energy and zeal Pan Macmillan soon established itself as one of the largest book publishers in the UK. By 2010, the advent of ebooks allowed the audience for popular fiction to grow dramatically, and Pan's bestselling authors, such as Peter James, Jeffrey Archer, Ken Follett and Kate Morton – not to mention bestselling saga writers Margaret Dickinson and Annie Murray – now reach an even wider readership.

Personally, my years working at Pan were incredibly exciting and a time of countless opportunities. The paperback market was exploding, and Pan was at the forefront. Sales were incredible – I remember selling close to a million copies of a Colin Dexter novella alone. I'm proud that today, Pan retains the same energy and vibrancy.

In the year that Pan celebrates its 70th anniversary its mission remains the same – to publish the best popular fiction and non-fiction for the widest audience.

David Macmillan

The Lady Vanishes

ETHEL LINA WHITE was born in Abergavenny in Monmouthshire, Wales, in 1876. She initially worked for the Ministry of Pensions but quit her job in order to write. She is the author of over fifteen mysteries and thrillers, several of which were made into films. *The Wheel Spins*, a masterpiece of suspense writing about a girl on a train, was immortalized by Alfred Hitchcock as *The Lady Vanishes*. Vastly successful in her day, White was as well-known as Agatha Christie and Dorothy L. Sayers, but fell into obscurity following her sudden death in 1944.

ETHEL LINA WHITE

The Lady Vanishes

PAN 70

First published 1936 by William Collins, Sons and Co. Ltd.
under the title *The Wheel Spins*

This edition published 2017 by Pan Books
an imprint of Pan Macmillan
20 New Wharf Road, London N1 9RR
Associated companies throughout the world
www.panmacmillan.com

ISBN 978-1-5098-5851-4

Pan Macmillan does not have any control over, or any responsibility for,
any author or third-party websites referred to in or on this book.

1 3 5 7 9 8 6 4 2

A CIP catalogue record for this book is available from the British Library.

Typeset by Palimpsest Book Production Ltd, Falkirk, Stirlingshire
Printed and bound by CPI Group (UK) Ltd, Croydon, CR0 4YY

The text of this book remains true to the original in every way.
Some aspects may appear out of date to modern-day readers, but are
reflective of the language and period in which they were originally written.
Macmillan believes changing the content to reflect today's world would
undermine the authenticity of the original, so has chosen to leave
the text in its entirety. This does not, however, constitute
an endorsement of the characterization and content.

Visit **www.panmacmillan.com** to read more about all our books
and to buy them. You will also find features, author interviews and
news of any author events, and you can sign up for e-newsletters
so that you're always first to hear about our new releases.

CHAPTER I

WITHOUT REGRETS

The day before the disaster, Iris Carr had her first premonition of danger. She was used to the protection of a crowd, whom—with unconscious flattery—she called "her friends." An attractive orphan of independent means, she had been surrounded always with clumps of people. They thought for her—or rather, she accepted their opinions, and they shouted for her—since her voice was rather too low in register, for mass social intercourse.

Their constant presence tended to create the illusion that she moved in a large circle, in spite of the fact that the same faces recurred with seasonal regularity. They also made her pleasantly aware of popularity. Her photograph appeared in the pictorial papers through the medium of a photographer's offer of publicity, after the Press announcement of her engagement to one of the crowd.

This was fame.

Then, shortly afterwards, her engagement was broken, by mutual consent—which was a lawful occasion for the reproduction of another portrait. More fame. And her mother, who died at her birth, might have wept or smiled at these pitiful flickers of human vanity, arising, like bubbles of marsh-gas, on the darkness below.

When she experienced her first threat of insecurity, Iris was feeling especially well and happy after an unconventional health-holiday. With the triumph of near-pioneers, the crowd had swooped down on a beautiful village of picturesque squalor, tucked away in a remote corner of Europe, and taken possession of it by the act of scrawling their names in the visitors' book.

For nearly a month they had invaded the only hotel, to the delighted demoralisation of the innkeeper and his staff. They scrambled up mountains, swam in the lake, and sunbathed on every available slope. When they were indoors, they filled the bar, shouted against the wireless, and tipped for each trifling service. The proprietor beamed at them over his choked cash-register, and the smiling waiters gave them preferential treatment, to the legitimate annoyance of the other English guests.

To these six persons, Iris appeared just one of her crowd, and a typical semi-Society girl—vain, selfish, and useless. Naturally, they had no knowledge of redeeming points—a generosity which made her accept the bill, as a matter of course, when she lunched with her "friends," and a real compassion for such cases of hardship which were clamped down under her eyes.

But while she was only vaguely conscious of fugitive moments of discontent and self-contempt, she was aware of a fastidious streak, which kept her aloof from any tendency to saturnalia. On this holiday she heard Pan's pipes, but had no experience of the kick of his hairy hindquarters.

Soon the slack convention of the crowd had been relaxed. They grew brown, they drank and were merry, while matrimonial boundaries became pleasantly blurred. Surrounded by a mixed bag of vague married couples, it was a sharp shock to Iris when one of the women—Olga—suddenly developed a belated sense of property, and accused her of stealing a husband.

Besides the unpleasantness of the scene, her sense of justice was outraged. She had merely tolerated a neglected male, who seemed a spare part in the dislocated domestic machine. It was not her fault that he had lost his head.

To make matters worse, at this crisis, she failed to notice any signs of real loyalty among her friends, who had plainly enjoyed the excitement. Therefore, to ease the tension, she decided not to travel back to England with the party, but to stay on for two days longer, alone.

She was still feeling sore, on the following day, when she accompanied the crowd to the little primitive railway station. They had already reacted to the prospect of a return to civilisation. They wore fashionable clothes again, and were roughly sorted into legitimate couples, as a natural sequence to the identification of suitcases and reservations.

The train was going to Trieste, which was definitely on the map. It was packed with tourists, who were also going back to pavements and lamp-posts. Forgetful of hillside and star-light, the crowd responded to the general noise and bustle. It seemed to recapture its old loyalty as it clustered round Iris.

"Sure you won't be bored, darling?"

"Change your mind and hop on."

"You've simply *got* to come."

As the whistle was blown, they tried to pull her into their carriage—just as she was, in shorts and nailed boots, and with a brown glaze of sunburn on her un-powdered face. She fought like a boxing-kangaroo to break free, and only succeeded in jumping down as the platform was beginning to slide past the window.

Laughing and panting from the struggle, she stood and waved after the receding train, until it disappeared round the bend of the gorge.

She felt almost guilty as she realised her relief at parting from her friends. But, although the holiday had been a success, she had drawn her pleasure chiefly from primeval sources—sun, water, and mountain-breeze. Steeped in Nature, she had vaguely resented the human intrusion.

They had all been together too closely and too intimately. At times, she had been conscious of jarring notes—a woman's high thin laugh—the tubby outline of a man's body, poised to dive—a continual flippant appeal to "My God."

It was true that while she had grown critical of her friends she had floated with the current. Like the others, she had raved of marvellous scenery, while she accepted it as a matter of course. It was a natural sequence that, when one travelled off the map, the landscape improved automatically as the standard of sanitation lapsed.

At last she was alone with the mountains and the silence. Below her lay a grass-green lake, sparkling with diamond reflections of the sun. The snowy peaks of distant ranges were silhouetted against a cornflower-blue sky. On a hill rose the dark pile of an ancient castle, with its five turrets pointing upwards, like the outspread fingers of a sinister hand.

Everywhere was a riot of colour. The station garden foamed with exotic flowers—flame and yellow—rising from spiked foliage. Higher up the slope, the small wooden hotel was painted ochre and crimson lake. Against the green wall of the gorge rose the last coil of smoke, like floating white feathers.

When it had faded away, Iris felt that the last link had been severed between her and the crowd. Blowing a derisive kiss, she turned away and clattered down the steep stony path. When she reached the glacier-fed river, she lingered on the bridge, to feel the iced air which arose from the greenish-white boil.

As she thought of yesterday's scene, she vowed that she never wanted to see the crowd again. They were connected with an episode which violated her idea of friendship. She had been a little fond of the woman, Olga, who had repaid her loyalty by a crude exhibition of jealousy.

She shrugged away the memory. Here, under the limitless blue, people seemed so small—their passions so paltry. They were merely incidental to the passage from the cradle to the grave. One met them and parted from them, without regrets.

Every minute the gap between her and them was widening. They were steaming away, out of her life. At the thought, she thrilled with a sense of new freedom, as though her spirit were liberated by the silence and solitude.

Yet, before many hours had passed, she would have bartered all the glories of Nature to have called them back again.

CHAPTER II

THE THREAT

Some four hours later Iris lay spread-eagled on a slope of the mountain, high above the valley. Ever since she had left the chill twilight of the gorge, at a shrine which marked a union of paths, she had been climbing steadily upwards, by a steep zigzag track.

After she had emerged from the belt of shadow, the sun had beat fiercely through her, but she did not slacken her pace. The fury of her thoughts drove her on, for she could not dislodge Olga from her mind.

The name was like a burr on her brain. *Olga.* Olga had eaten her bread, in the form of toast—for the sake of her figure—and had refused her salt, owing to a dietetic fad. This had made trouble in the kitchen. Olga had used her telephone, and mis-used her car. Olga had borrowed her fur coat, and had lent her a superfluous husband.

At the memory of Olga's Oscar, Iris put on a sprint.

"As if I'd skid for a man who looks like Mickey Mouse," she raged.

She was out of breath when, at last, she threw herself down on the turf and decided to call it a day. The mountain which had challenged her kept withdrawing as she advanced, so she had to give up her intention to reach the top.

As she lay with her eyes almost closed, listening to the ping of the breeze, her serenity returned. A clump of harebells, standing out against the skyline, seemed hardened and magnified to a metallic belfry, while she, herself, was dwarfed and welded into the earth—part of it, like the pebbles and the roots. In imagination she could almost hear the pumping of a giant heart underneath her head.

The moment passed, for she began to think of Olga again. This time, however, she viewed her from a different standpoint, for the altitude had produced the usual illusion of superiority. She reminded herself that the valley was four thousand feet above sea-level, while she had mounted about five thousand feet.

On the basis of this calculation she could afford to be generous, since she was nine thousand feet taller than her former friend—assuming, of course, that Olga was obliging enough to remain at sea-level.

She decided to wash out the memory as unworthy of further anger.

"But never again," she said. "After this, I'll never help anyone again."

Her voice had the passionate fervour of one who dedicates herself to some service. With the virtuous feeling of having profited by a lesson, for which heavy fees had been paid, she smoked a cigarette, before the return journey. The air was so clear that mountains she had never seen before quivered out of invisibility and floated in the sky, in mauve transparencies. Far below she could see an arm of the lake—no longer green, but dimmed by distance to a misted blue.

Reluctantly she rose to her feet. It was time to go.

The descent proved not only monotonous, but

painful, for the continual backward jolt of her weight threw a strain on unexercised muscles. Her calves began to ache and her toes were stubbed on the stony path.

Growing impatient, she decided to desert the zigzag in favour of a direct short-cut down the face of the mountain. With the lake as a guide to direction, she hurled herself down the slope.

It was a bold venture, but almost immediately she found that the gradient was too steep. As she was going too quickly to stop, her only course was to drop down to a sitting posture and glissade over the slippery turf—trusting to luck.

From that moment things happened quickly. Her pace increased every second, in spite of her efforts to brake with her feet. Patches of blue and green sped past her, as the valley rushed up to meet her, and smashed into the sky. Bumping over the rough ground, she steered towards a belt of trees at the bottom, in the hope that they might save her from a complete spill.

Unfortunately they proved to be rotten from age, and she crashed through them, to land with a bump in the middle of the stony pass.

Her fall had been partially broken, but she felt very sore and shaken as she scrambled to her feet. In spite of her injuries, she did not forget to give the forced laugh which had been drilled into her, at school, as the accompaniment to any games casualty.

"Rather amusing," she murmured, picking splinters out of her legs.

But she was pleased to notice the shrine, a few yards farther up the track, for this was a definite tribute to her steering. As she was not far from the hotel, she clattered down the gully, thinking of the comforts which awaited her. A long cold drink, a hot bath, dinner in bed. When she caught sight of a gleam of water, at the bend of the gorge, in her eagerness she broke into a limping run.

She rounded the corner and then stopped, staring before her in utter bewilderment. All the familiar landmarks had disappeared, as though some interfering person had passed an india-rubber over the landscape. There were no little wooden houses, no railway station, no pier, no hotel.

With a pang of dismay she realised that she had steered by a faulty compass. This was not their familiar green lake, in which she and her friends had bathed daily. Instead of being deep and ovoid in shape, it was a winding pale-blue mere, with shallow rushy margins.

In the circumstances, there was but one thing to do— retrace her steps back to the shrine and follow the other gully.

It was definitely amusing and she achieved quite a creditable laugh before she began to plod slowly upwards again.

Her mood was too bleak for her to appreciate the savage grandeur of the scenery. It was a scene of stark desolation, riven by landslips and piled high with shattered rocks. There was no crop of vegetation amid the boulders—no chirp of bird. The only sounds were the rattle of loose stones, dislodged by her feet, and the splash of a shrunken torrent, which foamed over its half-dried course, like a tangled white thread.

Used to perpetual company, Iris began to long for

faces and voices. In her loneliness, she was even reduced to the flabbiness of self-pity. She reminded herself that, when she returned to England, she would not go home, like others. She would merely go back.

At present she was living at an hotel, for she had sub-let her small luxury flat. Although her mode of living was her own choice, at such a time and such a place she felt that she paid a high price for freedom.

Her mood did not last, for, at the top of the pass, she was faced with a call upon her fortitude. Casting about, to pick up her bearings, she made the discovery that the shrine was different from the original landmark where she had struck the mountain zigzag.

This time she did not laugh, for she felt that humour could be carried too far. Instead she was furious with herself. She believed that she knew these mountains, because, with the others, she had clattered up and down the gorges, like a pack of wild goats.

But she had merely followed—while others led. Among the crowd was the inevitable leader—the youth with the map.

Thrown on her own resources, she had not the least idea of her direction. All she could do was to follow the gorge up to its next ramification and trust to luck.

"If I keep on walking, I must get somewhere," she argued. "Besides, no one can get lost who has a tongue."

She had need of her stoicism, for she had grown desperately weary, in addition to the handicap of a sore heel. When, at last, she reached a branch which gave her a choice of roads, she was too distrustful of her own judgment to experiment. Sitting down on a boulder, she waited on the chance of hailing some passer-by.

It was her zero-hour, when her independence appeared only the faculty to sign cheques drawn on money made by others—and her popularity, but a dividend of the same cheques.

"I've been carried all my life," she thought. "And even if some one comes, I'm the world's worst linguist."

The description flattered her, for she had not the slightest claim to the title of linguist. Her ignorance of foreign languages was the result of being finished at Paris and Dresden. During the time she was at school, she mixed exclusively with other English girls, while the natives who taught her acquired excellent English accents.

This was her rendering of the line in the National Anthem—"Send us victorious."

Patriotism did not help her now, for she felt slightly doubtful when a thick-set swarthy man, wearing leather shorts and dirty coloured braces, swung up the pass.

Among Iris' crowd was a youth who was clever at languages. From his knowledge of common roots, he had managed to use German as a kind of liaison language; but he had to draw on his imagination in order to interpret and be understood.

Iris had a vivid recollection of how the crowd used to hoot with derision at his failures, when she called out to the man in English and asked him to direct her to the village.

He stared at her, shrugged, and shook his head.

Her second attempt—in a louder key—met with no

better success. The peasant, who seemed in a hurry, was passing on, when Iris barred his way.

She was acutely aware of her own impotence, as though she were some maimed creature, whose tongue had been torn out. But she had to hold his attention, to compel him to understand. Feeling that she had lapsed from the dignity of a rational being, she was forced to make pantomimic gestures, pointing to the alternative routes in turn, while she kept repeating the name of the village.

"He must get that, unless he's an idiot," she thought.

The man seemed to grasp her drift, for he nodded several times. But, instead of indicating any direction, he broke into an unfamiliar jargon.

As Iris listened to the torrent of guttural sounds, her nerve snapped suddenly. She felt cut off from all human intercourse, as though a boundary-line had been wiped out, and—instead of being in Europe—she were stranded in a corner of Asia.

Without money and without a common language, she could wander indefinitely. At that moment she might be headed away from the village and into the wilds. The gorge had many tributary, branches, like the windings of an inland sea.

As she grew afraid, the peasant's face began to waver, like the illusion of some bad dream. She noticed that his skin glistened and that he had a slight goitre; but she was definitely conscious of his steamy goatish smell, for he was sweating from his climb.

"I can't understand you," she cried hysterically. "I

can't understand one word. Stop. Oh, *stop*. You'll drive me mad."

In his turn the man heard only a string of gibberish. He saw a girl, dressed like a man, who was unattractively skinny—according to the local standard of beauty—with cut dirty knees. She was a foreigner, although he did not know her nationality. Further, she was worked up to a pitch of excitement, and was exceptionally stupid.

She did not seem to grasp that she was telling him less than half the name of the village, whereas three different hamlets had the same prefix. He had explained this to her, and asked for the full word.

Iris could not have supplied it even if she had understood the man. The name of the village was such a tongue-twister that she had never tried to disentangle it, but, like the rest, had called it by its first three syllables.

The position was stalemate. With a final grimace and shrug, the peasant went on his way, leaving Iris alone with the mountains.

They overhung her like a concrete threat. She had bought picture-postcards of them and broadcast them with the stereotyped comment—"Marvellous scenery." Once she had even scrawled "This is my room," and marked a peak with a derisive cross.

Now—the mountains were having their revenge. As she cowered under the projecting cliffs, she felt they had but to shake those towering brows, to crush her to powder beneath an avalanche of boulders. They dwarfed her to insignificance. They blotted out her individuality. They extinguished her spirit.

The spell was broken by the sound of English voices.

Round the bend of the pass came the honeymoon couple, from the hotel.

This pair of lovers was respected even by the crowd, for the completeness of their reserve and the splendour of their appearance. The man was tall, handsome, and of commanding carriage. His voice was authoritative, and he held his head at an angle which suggested excessive pride. Waiters scampered at his nod, and the innkeeper—probably on the strength of his private sitting-room—called him "Milord."

His wife was almost as tall, with a perfect figure and a flawless face. She wore beautiful clothes which were entirely unsuitable for the wilds; but it was obvious that she dressed thus as a matter of course, and to please only her husband.

They set their own standard and appeared unconscious of the other visitors, who accepted them as belonging to a higher social sphere. It was suspected that the name "Todhunter," under which they had registered, was a fiction to preserve their anonymity.

They passed Iris almost without notice. The man raised his hat vaguely, but his glance held no recognition. His wife never removed her violet eyes from the stony track, for her heels were perilously high.

She was speaking in a low voice, which was vehement in spite of its muffled tone.

"No, darling. Not another day. Not even for *you*. We've stayed too—"

Iris lost the rest of the sentence. She prepared to follow them at a discreet distance, for she had become acutely aware of her own wrecked appearance.

The arrival of the honeymoon pair had restored her sense of values. Their presence was proof that the hotel was not far away, for they never walked any distance. At the knowledge, the mountains shrank back to camera-subjects, while she was reconstructed, from a lost entity to a London girl who was critical about the cut of her shorts.

Very soon she recognised the original shrine, whence she had deserted the pass. Limping painfully down the track, presently she caught the gleam of the darkening lake and the lights of the hotel, shining through the green gloom.

She began to think again of a hot bath and dinner as she remembered that she was both tired and hungry.

But although apparently only the physical traces of her adventure remained, actually her sense of security had been assailed—as if the experience were a threat from the future, to reveal the horror of helplessness, far away from all that was familiar.

CHAPTER III

CONVERSATION PIECE

When the honeymoon pair returned to the hotel the four remaining guests were sitting outside on the gravelled square, before the veranda. They were enjoying the restful interlude of "between the lights." It was too dark to write letters, or read—too early to dress for dinner. Empty cups and cake-crumbs on one of the tables showed that they had taken afternoon tea in the open and had not moved since.

It was typical of two of them, the Misses Flood-Porter, to settle. They were not the kind that flitted, being in the fifties and definitely set in their figures and their habits. Both had immaculately waved grey hair, which retained sufficient samples of the original tint to give them the courtesy-title of blondes. They had also, in common, excellent natural complexions and rather fierce expressions.

The delicate skin of the elder—Miss Evelyn—was slightly shrivelled, for she was nearly sixty, while Miss Rose was only just out of the forties. The younger sister was taller and stouter; her voice was louder, her colour deeper. In an otherwise excellent character, was a streak of amiable bully, which made her inclined to scold her partner at contract.

During their visit, they had formed a quartette with the Reverend Kenneth Barnes and his wife. They had travelled out on the same train, and they planned to return to England together. The vicar and his wife had the gift of pleasant companionship, which the Misses Flood-Porter—who were without it—attributed to mutual tastes and prejudices.

The courtyard was furnished with iron chairs and tables, enamelled in brilliant colours, and was decorated with tubs of dusty evergreen shrubs. As Miss Flood-Porter looked around her, she thought of her own delightful home in a Cathedral city.

According to the papers, there had been rain in England, so the garden should look its best, with vivid green grass and lush borders of asters and dahlias.

"I'm looking forward to seeing my garden again," she said.

"Ours," corrected her sister, who was John Blunt.

"And I'm looking forward to a comfortable chair," laughed the vicar. "Ha! Here comes the bridal pair."

In spite of a sympathetic interest in his fellows he did not call out a genial greeting. He had learned from his first—and final—rebuff that they resented any intrusion on their privacy. So he leaned back, puffing at his pipe, while he watched them mount the steps of the veranda.

"Handsome pair," he said in an approving voice.

"I wonder who they *really* are," remarked Miss Flood-Porter. "The man's face is familiar to me. I know I've seen him somewhere."

"On the pictures, perhaps," suggested her sister.

"Oh, do you go?" broke in Mrs. Barnes eagerly, hoping to claim another taste in common, for she concealed a guilty passion for the cinema.

"Only to see George Arliss and Diana Wynyard," explained Miss Flood-Porter.

"That settles it," said the vicar. "He's certainly not George Arliss, and neither is she Diana."

"All the same, I feel certain there is some mystery about them," persisted Miss Flood-Porter.

"So do I," agreed Mrs. Barnes. "I—I wonder if they are really married."

"Are *you*?" asked her husband quickly.

He laughed gently when his wife flushed to her eyes.

"Sorry to startle you, my dear," he said, "but isn't it simpler to believe that we are all of us what we assume to be? Even parsons and their wives." He knocked the ashes out of his pipe, and rose from his chair. "I think I'll stroll down to the village for a chat with my friends."

"How can he talk to them when he doesn't know their language?" demanded Miss Rose bluntly, when the vicar had gone from the garden.

"Oh, he *makes* them understand," explained his wife proudly. "Sympathy, you know, and common humanity. He'd rub noses with a savage."

"I'm afraid we drove him away by talking scandal," said Miss Flood-Porter.

"It was my fault," declared Mrs. Barnes. "I know people think I'm curious. But, really, I have to force myself to show an interest in my neighbour's affairs. It's my protest against our terrible national shyness."

"But we're proud of that," broke in Miss Rose. "England does not need to advertise."

"Of course not. . . . But we only pass this way once. I have to remind myself that the stranger sitting beside me may be in some trouble and that I might be able to help."

The sisters looked at her with approval. She was a slender woman in the mid-forties, with a pale oval face, dark hair, and a sweet expression. Her large brown eyes were both kind and frank—her manner sincere.

It was impossible to connect her with anything but rigid honesty. They knew that she floundered into awkward explanations, rather than run the risk of giving a false impression.

In her turn, she liked the sisters. They were of solid worth and sound respectability. One felt that they would serve on juries with distinction, and do their duty to their God and their neighbour—while permitting no direction as to its nature.

They were also leisured people, with a charming house and garden, well-trained maids and frozen assets in the bank. Mrs. Barnes knew this, so, being human, it gave her a feeling of superiority to reflect that the one man in their party was her husband.

She could appreciate the sense of ownership, because, up to her fortieth birthday, she had gone on her yearly holiday in the company of a huddle of other spinsters. Since she had left school, she had earned her living by teaching, until the miracle happened which gave her—not only a husband—but a son.

Both she and her husband were so wrapped up in the child, that the vicar sometimes feared that their devotion was tempting Fate. The night before they set out on their holiday he proposed a pact.

"Yes," he agreed, looking down at the sleeping boy in

his cot. "He *is* beautiful. But . . . It is my privilege to read the Commandments to others. Sometimes, I wonder—"

"I know what you mean," interrupted his wife. "Idolatry."

He nodded.

"I am as guilty as you," he admitted. "So I mean to discipline myself. In our position, we have special opportunities to influence others. We must not grow lop-sided, but develop every part of our nature. If this holiday is to do us real good, it *must* be a complete mental change. . . . My dear, suppose we agree not to talk exclusively of Gabriel, while we are away?"

Mrs. Barnes agreed. But her promise did not prevent her from thinking of him continually. Although they had left him in the care of a competent grandmother, she was foolishly apprehensive about his health.

While she was counting the remaining hours before her return to her son, and Miss Flood-Porter smiled in anticipation of seeing her garden, Miss Rose was pursuing her original train of thought. She always ploughed a straight furrow, right to its end.

"I can't understand how anyone can tell a lie," she declared. "Unless, perhaps, some poor devil who's afraid of being sacked. But—people like *us*. We know a wealthy woman who boasts of making false declarations at the Customs. Sheer dishonesty."

As she spoke, Iris appeared at the gate of the hotel garden. She did her best to skirt the group at the table, but she could not avoid hearing what was said.

"Perhaps I should not judge others," remarked Mrs.

Barnes in the clear carrying voice of a form-mistress. "I've never felt the slightest temptation to tell a lie."

"Liar," thought Iris automatically.

She was in a state of utter fatigue, which bordered on collapse. It was only by the exercise of every atom of will-power that she forced herself to reach the hotel. The ordeal had strained her nerves almost to breaking-point. Although she longed for the quiet of her room, she knew she could not mount the stairs without a short rest. Every muscle felt wrenched as she dropped down on an iron chair and closed her eyes.

"If anyone speaks to me, I'll scream," she thought.

The Misses Flood-Porter exchanged glances and turned down the corners of their mouths. Even gentle Mrs. Barnes' soft brown eyes held no welcome, for she had been a special victim of the crowd's bad manners and selfishness.

They behaved as though they had bought the hotel and the other guests were interlopers, exacting preferential treatment—and getting it—by bribery. This infringement of fair-dealing annoyed the other tourists, as they adhered to the terms of their payment to a travelling agency, which included service.

The crowd monopolised the billiard-table and secured the best chairs. They were always served first at meals; courses gave out, and bath-water ran lukewarm.

Even the vicar found that his charity was strained. He did his best to make allowance for the animal spirits of youth, although he was aware that several among the party could not be termed juvenile.

Unfortunately, Iris' so-called friends included two

persons who were no testimonial for the English nation; and since it was difficult to distinguish one girl in a bathing-brief from another, Mrs. Barnes was of the opinion that they were all doing the same thing—getting drunk and making love.

Her standard of decency was offended by the sun-bathing—her nights disturbed by noise. Therefore she was specially grateful for the prospect of two peaceful days, spent amid glorious scenery and in congenial company.

But, apparently, there was not a complete clearance of the crowd; there was a hangover, in this girl—and there might be others. Mrs. Barnes had vaguely remarked Iris, because she was pretty and had been pursued by a bathing-gentleman with a matronly figure.

As the man was married, his selection was not to her credit. But she seemed to be so exhausted that Mrs. Barnes' kindly heart soon reproached her for lack of sympathy.

"Are you left all alone?" she called, in her brightest tones.

Iris shuddered at the unexpected overture. At that moment the last thing in the world she wanted was mature interest, which, in her experience, masked curiosity.

"Yes," she replied.

"Oh, dear, what a shame. Aren't you lonely?"

"No."

"But you're rather young to be travelling without friends. Couldn't any of your people come with you?"

"I have none."

"No family at all?"

"No, and no relatives. Aren't I lucky?"

Iris was not near enough to hear the horrified gasp of the Misses Flood-Porter; but Mrs. Barnes' silence told her that her snub had not miscarried. To avoid a further inquisition, she made a supreme effort to rise, for she was stiffening in every joint, and managed to drag herself into the hotel and upstairs to her room.

Mrs. Barnes tried to carry off the incident with a laugh.

"I'm afraid I've blundered again," she said. "She plainly resented me. But it seemed hardly human for us to sit like dummies, and show no interest in her."

"Is she interested in *you*?" demanded Miss Rose. "Or in us? That sort of girl is utterly selfish. She wouldn't raise a finger, or go an inch out of her way, to help anyone."

There was only one answer to the question, which Mrs. Barnes was too kind to make. So she remained silent, since she could not tell a lie.

Neither she—nor any one else—could foretell the course of the next twenty-four hours, when this girl—standing alone against a cloud of witnesses—would endure such anguish of spirit as threatened her sanity, on behalf of a stranger for whom she had no personal feeling.

Or rather—if there was actually such a person as Miss Froy.

CHAPTER IV

ENGLAND GALLING

Because she had a square on her palm, which, according to a fortune-teller, signified safety, Iris believed that she lived in a protected area. Although she laughed at the time, she was impressed secretly, because hers was a specially sheltered life.

At this crisis, the stars, as usual, seemed to be fighting for her. The mountains had sent out a preliminary warning. During the evening, too, she received overtures of companionship, which might have delivered her from mental isolation.

Yet she deliberately cut every strand which linked her with safety, out of mistaken loyalty to her friends.

She missed them directly she entered the lounge, which was silent and deserted. As she walked along the corridor, she passed empty bedrooms, with stripped beds and littered floors. Mattresses hung from every window and the small verandas were heaped with pillows.

It was not only company which was lacking, but moral support. The crowd never troubled to change for the evening, unless comfort suggested flannel trousers. On one occasion, it had achieved the triumph of a complaint, when a lady appeared at dinner dressed in her bathing-slip.

The plaintiffs had been the Misses Flood-Porter, who always wore expensive but sober dinner-gowns. Iris remembered the incident, when she had finished her bath. Although slightly ashamed of her deference to public opinion, she fished from a suitcase an unpacked afternoon frock of crinkled crêpe.

The hot soak and rest had refreshed her, but she felt lonely, as she leaned over the balustrade. Her pensive pose and the graceful lines of her dress arrested the attention of the bridegroom—Todhunter, according to the register—as he strolled out of his bedroom.

He had not the least knowledge of her identity, or that he had acted as a sort of guiding-star to her in the gorge. He and his wife took their meals in their private sitting-room and never mingled with the crowd. He concluded, therefore, that she was an odd guest whom he had missed in the general scramble.

Approving her with an experienced eye, he stopped.

"Quiet, to-night," he remarked. "Refreshing change after the din of that horrible rabble."

To his surprise, the girl looked coldly at him.

"It *is* quiet," she said. "But I happen to miss my friends."

As she walked downstairs she felt defiantly glad that she had made him realise his blunder. Championship of her friends mattered more than the absence of social sense. But, in spite of her triumph, the incident was vaguely unpleasant.

The crowd had gloried in its unpopularity, which seemed to it a sign of superiority. It frequently remarked in complacent voices, "We're not popular with these people," or "They don't really like us." Under the influence of its mass-hypnotism, Iris wanted no other label.

But now that she was alone, it was not quite so amusing to realise that the other guests, who were presumably decent and well-bred, considered her an outsider.

Her mood was bleakly defiant when she entered the restaurant. It was a big bare room, hung with stiff deep-blue wallpaper, patterned with conventional gilt stars. The electric lights were set in clumsy wrought-iron chandeliers, which suggested a Hollywood set for a medieval castle. Scarcely any of the tables were laid, and only one waiter drooped at the door.

In a few days, the hotel would be shut up for the winter. With the departure of the big English party, most of the holiday staff had become superfluous and had already gone back to their homes in the district.

The remaining guests appeared to be unaffected by the air of neglect and desolation inseparable from the end of the season. The Misses Flood-Porter shared a table with the vicar and his wife. They were all in excellent spirits and gave the impression of having come into their own, as they capped each other's jokes, culled from *Punch*.

Iris pointedly chose a small table in a far corner. She smoked a cigarette while she waited to be served. The others were advanced in their meal and it was a novel sensation for one of the crowd to be in arrears.

Mrs. Barnes, who was too generous to nurse resentment for her snub, looked at her with admiring eyes.

"How pretty that girl looks in a frock!" she said.

"*Afternoon* frock," qualified Miss Flood-Porter. "We always make a point of wearing evening dress for dinner, when we're on the Continent."

"If we didn't dress, we should feel we were letting England down," explained the younger sister.

Although Iris span out her meal to its limit, she was driven back ultimately to the lounge. She was too tired to stroll and it was early for bed. As she looked around her, she could hardly believe that, only the night before, it had been a scene of continental glitter and gaiety—although the latter quality had been imported from England. Now that it was no longer filled with her friends, she was shocked to notice its tawdry theatrical finery. The gilt cane chairs were tarnished, the crimson plush upholstery shabby.

A clutter of cigarette stubs and spent matches in the palm pots brought a lump to her throat. They were all that remained of the crowd.

As she sat apart, the vicar—pipe in mouth—watched her with a thoughtful frown. His clear-cut face was both strong and sensitive, and an almost perfect blend of flesh and spirit. He played rough football with the youths of his parish, and, afterwards, took their souls by assault; but he had also a real understanding of the problems of his women-parishioners.

When his wife told him of Iris' wish for solitude, he could enter into her feeling, because, sometimes, he yearned to escape from people and even from his wife. His own inclination was to leave her to the boredom of her own company; yet he was touched by the dark lines under her eyes and her mournful lips.

In the end, he resolved to ease his conscience at the cost of a rebuff. He knew it was coming, because, as he crossed the lounge, she looked up quickly, as though on guard.

"Another," she thought.

From a distance she had admired the spirituality or his expression; but to-night he was numbered among her hostile critics.

"Horrible rabble." The words floated into her memory, as he spoke to her.

"If you are travelling back to England alone, would you care to join our party?"

"When are you going?" she asked.

"Day after to-morrow, before they take off the last through train of the season."

"But I'm going to-morrow. Thanks so much."

"Then I'll wish you a pleasant journey."

The vicar smiled faintly at her lightning decision as he crossed to a table and began to address luggage-labels.

His absence was his wife's opportunity. In her wish not to break her promise, she had gone to the other extreme and had not mentioned her baby to her new friends, save for one casual allusion to "our little boy." But, now that the holiday was nearly over, she could not resist the temptation of showing his photograph, which had won a prize in a local baby competition.

With a guilty glance at her husband's back she drew out of her bag a limp leather case.

"This is my large son," she said, trying to hide her pride.

The Misses Flood-Porter were exclusive animal-lovers and not particularly fond of children. But they said all the correct things with such well-bred conviction that Mrs. Barnes' heart swelled with triumph.

Miss Rose, however, switched off to another subject directly the vicar returned from the writing-table.

"Do you believe in warning dreams, Mr. Barnes?" she asked. "Because, last night, I dreamed of a railway smash."

The question caught Iris' attention and she strained to hear the vicar's reply.

"I'll answer your question," he said, "if you'll first answer mine. What *is* a dream? Is it stifled apprehension—"

"I wonder," said a bright voice in Iris' ear, "I wonder if you would like to see the photograph of my little son, Gabriel?"

Iris realised dimly that Mrs. Barnes—who was keeping up England in limp brown lace—had seated herself beside her and was showing her the photograph of a naked baby.

She made a pretence of looking at it while she tried to listen to the vicar.

"Gabriel," she repeated vaguely.

"Yes, after the Archangel. We named him after him."

"How sweet! Did he send a mug?"

Mrs. Barnes stared incredulously, while her sensitive face grew scarlet. She believed that the girl had been intentionally profane and had insulted her precious little son, to avenge her boredom. Pressing her trembling lips together she rejoined her friends.

Iris was grateful when the humming in her ears ceased. She was unaware of her slip, because she had only caught a fragment of Mrs. Barnes' explanation. Her interest was still held by the talk of presentiments.

"Say what you like," declared Miss Rose, sweeping away the vicar's argument, "I've common sense on my side. They usually try to pack too many passengers into the last good train of the season. I know I'll be precious glad when I'm safely back in England."

A spirit of apprehension quivered in the air at her words.

"But you aren't really afraid of an accident?" cried Mrs. Barnes, clutching Gabriel's photograph tightly.

"Of course not." Miss Flood-Porter answered for her sister. "Only, perhaps we feel we're rather off the beaten track here, and so very far from home. Our trouble is we don't know a word of the language."

"She means," cut in Miss Rose, "we're all right over reservations and coupons, so long as we stick to hotels and trains. But if some accident happened to make us break our journey, or lose a connection, and we were stranded in some small place, we should feel *lost*. Besides it would be awkward about money. We didn't bring any travellers' cheques."

The elder sister appealed to the vicar.

"Do you advise us to take my sister's dream as a warning and travel back to-morrow?"

"No, *don't*," murmured Iris under her breath.

She waited for the vicar's answer with painful interest, for she was not eager to travel on the same train as these uncongenial people, who might feel it their duty to befriend her.

"You must follow your own inclination," said the

vicar. "But if you do leave prematurely, you will not only give a victory to superstition, but you will deprive yourself of another day in these glorious surroundings."

"And our reservations are for the day after tomorrow," remarked Miss Rose. "We'd better not risk any muddles. . . . And now, I'm going up to pack for my journey back to dear old England."

To the surprise of every one her domineering voice suddenly blurred with emotion. Miss Flood-Porter waited until she had gone out of the lounge, before she explained.

"Nerves. We had a very trying experience, just before we came away. The doctor ordered a complete change so we came here, instead of Switzerland."

Then the innkeeper came in, and, as a compliment to his guests, fiddled with his radio, until he managed to get London on the long wave. Amid a machine-gun rattle of atmospherics, a familiar mellow voice informed them, "You have just been listening to . . ."

But they had heard nothing.

Miss Flood-Porter saw her garden, silvered by the harvest moon. She wondered whether the chrysanthemum buds, three to a pot, were swelling, and if the blue salvias had escaped the slugs.

Miss Rose, briskly stacking shoes in the bottom of a suitcase, quivered at a recollection. Again she saw a gaping hole in a garden-bed, where overnight had stood a cherished clump of white delphiniums. . . . It was not only the loss of their treasure, but the nerve-racking ignorance of where the enemy would strike next . . .

The vicar and his wife thought of their baby, asleep

31

in his cot. They must decide whether they should merely peep at him, or risk waking him with a kiss.

Iris remembered her friends in the roaring express and was suddenly smitten with a wave of home-sickness.

England was calling.

CHAPTER V

THE NIGHT EXPRESS

Iris was awakened that night, as usual, by the express screaming through the darkness. Jumping out of bed, she reached the window in time to see it outline the curve of the lake with a fiery wire. As it rattled below the hotel, the golden streak expanded to a string of lighted windows, which, when it passed, snapped together again like the links of a bracelet.

After it had disappeared around the gorge, she followed its course by its pall of quivering red smoke. In imagination, she saw it shooting through Europe, as though it were an explosive shuttle ripping through the scorched fabric of the map. It caught up cities and threaded them on a gleaming whistling string. Illuminated names flashed before her eyes and were gone—Bucharest, Zagreb, Trieste, Milan, Basle, Calais.

Once again she was flooded with home-hunger, even though her future address were an hotel. Mixed with it was a gust of foreboding—which was a legacy from the mountains.

"Suppose—something—happened, and I never came back."

At that moment she felt that any evil could block the way to her return. A railway crash, illness, or crime were possibilities, which were actually scheduled in other lives. They were happening all around her and at any time a line might give way in the protective square in her palm.

As she lay and tossed, she consoled herself with the reminder that this was the last time she would lie under the lumpy feather bed. Throughout the next two nights she, too, would be rushing through dark landscape, jerked out of every brief spell of sleep by the flash of lights, whenever the express roared through a station.

The thought was with her when she woke, the next morning, to see the silhouette of mountain-peaks iced against the flush of sunrise.

"I'm going home to-day," she told herself exultantly.

The air was raw when she looked out of her window. Mist was rising from the lake which gleamed greenly through yellowed fans of chestnut trees. But in spite of the blue and gold glory of autumn she felt indifferent to its beauty.

She was also detached from the drawbacks of her room, which usually offended her critical taste. Its wooden walls were stained a crude shade of raw sienna, and instead of running water there was a battered wash-stand which bore a tin can, covered with a thin towel.

In spirit, Iris had already left the hotel. Her journey was begun before she started. When she went down to the restaurant she was barely conscious of the other guests, who, only a few hours before, had inspired her with antipathy.

The Misses Flood-Porter, who were dressed for writing letters in the open, were breakfasting at a table by the window. They did not speak to her, although they would have bowed as a matter of courtesy, had they caught her eye.

Iris did not notice the omission, because they had

gone completely out of her life. She drank her coffee in a silence which was broken by occasional remarks from the sisters, who wondered whether the English weather were kind for a local military wedding.

Her luck held, for she was spared contact with the other guests, who were engrossed by their own affairs. As she passed the bureau, Mrs. Barnes was calling a waiter's attention to a letter in one of the pigeon-holes. Her grey jersey-suit, as well as her packet of sandwiches, advertised an excursion.

The vicar, who was filling his pipe on the veranda, was also in unconventional kit—shorts, sweater, nailed boots, and the local felt hat—adorned with a tiny blue feather—which he had bought as a souvenir of his holiday.

His smile was so happy that Iris thought he looked both festive and good, as though a saint had deserted his shrine, knocking his halo a trifle askew in the process, in order to put a coat of sunburn over his pallid plaster.

Her tolerance faded as she listened to a dialogue which was destined to affect her own future.

"Is that a letter from home?" called the vicar.

"Yes," replied his wife, after a pause.

"I thought Grandma told us to expect no more letters. . . . What's she writing about?"

"She wants me to do a little shopping for her, on our way through London. Some Margaret Rose silk. The little Princess, you know."

"But you'll be tired. It's not very considerate."

"No." Mrs. Barnes voice was exceptionally sharp. "It's *not*. Why didn't she *think*?"

Iris condoned her own ungracious conduct of the preceding night, as she left them to their discussion. She told herself that she was justified in protecting herself from the boredom of domestic trifles.

As she strolled past the front of the hotel, she had to draw back to avoid trespassing on the privacy of the honeymoon pair, whose sitting-room opened on to the veranda. They were breakfasting in the open air, off rolls and fruit. The man was resplendent in a Chinese dressing-gown, while his wife wore an elaborate wrapper over satin pyjamas.

The Todhunters annoyed Iris, because they affected her with vague discontent. She was conscious of the same unacknowledged blank when she watched a love-scene played by two film stars. Theirs was passion— perfectly dressed, discreetly censored and with the better profile presented to the camera.

She felt a responsive thrill when the man looked into his bride's eyes with intense personal interest.

"Has it been perfect?" he asked.

Mrs. Todhunter knew exactly how long to pause before her reply.

"Yes."

It was faultless timing for he understood what she did not say.

"*Not* perfect, then," he remarked. "But, darling, is anything—"

Iris passed out of earshot, while she was still slightly envious. Her own experience of love had been merely a succession of episodes which led up to the photographic farce of her engagement.

The morning seemed endless, but at length it wore away. She had little to pack, because—following tradition—her friends had taken the bulk of her luggage with them, to save her trouble. An hour or two were killed, or rather drowned, in the lake, but she was too impatient to lie in the sun.

After she had changed for her journey, she went down to the restaurant. The dish of the day was attractively jellied and garnished with sprigs of tarragon, chervil, and chopped eggs; but she suspected that it was composed of poached eels. Turning away, with a shudder, she took possession of a small buttercup-painted table in the gravelled garden, where she lunched on potato-soup and tiny grapes.

The sun flickered through the dense roof of chestnuts, but the iron chair was too hard and cold for comfort. Although the express was not due for more than an hour, she decided to wait for it at the railway station where she could enjoy a view.

She had worked herself up to a fever, so that the act of leaving the hotel seemed to bring her a step nearer to her journey. It gave her acute pleasure to pay her bill and tip the stragglers of the staff. Although she saw none of her fellow-guests, she hurried through the garden, like a truant from school, as though she feared she might be detained, at the last minute.

It was strange to wear a sophisticated travelling-suit and high heels again, as she jolted down the rough path, followed by a porter with her baggage. The sensation was not too comfortable after weeks of liberty, but she welcomed it as part of her return to civilisation. When she was seated on the platform, her suitcase at her feet, and the shimmer of the lake below, she was conscious of having reached a peak of enjoyment.

The air was water-clear and held the sting of altitude. As the sun blazed down on her, she felt steeped in warmth and drenched in light. She took off her hat and gazed at the signal post, anticipating the thrill of its drop, followed by the first glimpse of a foreshortened engine at the end of the rails.

There were other people on the platform, for the arrival of the express was the main event of the day. It was too early for the genuine travellers, but groups of loiterers, both visitors and natives, hung around the fruit and paper-stalls. They were a cheerful company and noisy in many languages. Iris heard no English until two men came down the road from the village.

They leaned over the palings behind her, to continue an argument. She did not feel sufficient interest, at first, to turn and see their faces, but their voices were so distinctive that, presently, she could visualise them.

The one whom she judged the younger had an eager untidy voice. She felt sure that he possessed an active brain, with a rush of ideas. He spoke too quickly and often stumbled for a word, probably not because his terms were limited, but because he had a choice of too many.

Gradually he won her sympathy, partly because his mind seemed in tune—or rather, in discord—with hers and partly because she disliked the other speaker instinctively. His accent was pedantic and consciously cultured.

He spoke deliberately, with an irritating authority, which betrayed his inflexible mind.

"Oh, no, my dear Hare." Iris felt it should have been "Watson." "You're abysmally wrong. It has been proved conclusively that there can be no fairer or better system of justice than trial by jury."

"Trial by fatheads," spluttered the younger voice. "You talk of ordinary citizens. No one is ordinary, but a bag of his special prejudices. One woman's got a spite against her sex—one man's cranky on morality. They all damn the prisoner on different issues. And they've all businesses or homes which they want to get back to. They watch the clock and grasp the obvious."

"They are directed by the judge."

"And how much of his direction do they remember? You know how your own mind slips when you're listening to a string of words. Besides, after he's dotted all the i's and crossed the t's for them, they stampede and bring him in the wrong verdict."

"Why should you assume it is wrong? They have formed their own conclusion on the testimony of the witnesses."

"*Witnesses.*" In his heat the young man thumped the railing. "The witness is the most damnable part of the outfit. He may be so stupid as to be putty in the hands of some wily lawyer, or he may be smart and lie away some wretched man's life, just to read about his own wonderful memory and powers of observation and see his photograph in the papers. They're all out for publicity."

The elder man laughed in a superior manner which irritated his companion to the personal touch.

"When I'm accused of bumping you off, Professor, I'd rather be tried by a team of judges who'd bring trained legal minds and impartial justice to bear on the facts."

"You're biased," said the Professor. ". . . Let me try to convince you. The jury is intelligent in bulk, and can judge character. Certain witnesses are reliable, while others must be viewed with suspicion. For instance, how would you describe that dark woman with the artificial lashes?"

"Attractive."

"Hum. *I* should call her meretricious and so would any average man of the world. Now, we'll assume that she and that English lady in the Burberry are giving contrary evidence. One of the two must be telling a lie."

"I don't agree. It may depend on the point of view. The man in the street, with his own back garden, is ready to swear to lilac when he sees it; but when he goes to a botanical garden he finds it's labelled syringa."

"The generic name—"

"I know, *I* know. But if one honest John Citizen swears syringa is white, while another swears it's mauve, you'll grant that there is an opportunity for confusion. Evidence may be like that."

"Haven't you wandered from my point?" asked the conventional voice. "Put those two women, separately, into the witness-box. Now *which* are you going to believe?"

In her turn, Iris compared the hypothetical witnesses.

One was a characteristic type of county Englishwoman, with an athletic figure and a pleasant intelligent face. If she strode across the station as though she possessed the right of way, she used it merely as a short cut to her legitimate goal.

On the other hand, the pretty dark woman was an obvious loiterer. Her skin-tight skirt and embroidered peasant blouse might have been the holiday attire of any continental lady; but, in spite of her attractive red lips and expressive eyes, Iris could not help thinking of a gipsy who had just stolen a chicken for the pot.

Against her will, she had to agree with the Professor. Yet she felt almost vexed with the younger man when he ceased to argue, because she had backed the losing side.

"I see your point," he said. "The British waterproof wins every time. But Congo rubber was a bloody business and too wholesale a belief in rubber-proofing may lead to a bloody mix-up. . . . Come and have a drink."

"Thank you, if you will allow me to order it. I wish to avail myself of every opportunity of speaking the language."

"Wish I could forget it. It's a disgusting one—all spitting and sneezing. You lecture on Modern Languages, don't you? Many girl students in your classes?"

"Yes. . . . Unfortunately."

Iris was sorry when they moved away, for she had been idly interested in their argument. The crowd on the platform had increased, although the express was not due for another twenty-five minutes, even if it ran to time. She had now to share her bench with others, while a child squatted on her suitcase.

Although spoiled by circumstances she did not resent the intrusion. The confusion could not touch her, because she was held by the moment. The glow of sunshine, the green flicker of trees, the gleam of the lake, all combined to hypnotise her to a condition of stationary bliss.

There was nothing to warn her of the attack. When she least expected it, the blow fell.

Suddenly she felt a violent pain at the back of her neck. Almost before she realised it, the white-capped mountains rocked, the blue sky turned black, and she dropped down into darkness.

CHAPTER VI

THE WAITING-ROOM

When Iris became conscious, her sight returned, at first, in patches. She saw sections of faces floating in the air. It seemed the same face—sallow-skinned, with black eyes and bad teeth.

Gradually she realised that she was lying on a bench in a dark kind of shed while a ring of women surrounded her. They were of peasant type, with a racial resemblance accentuated by inter-marriage.

They stared down at her with indifferent apathy, as though she were some street spectacle—a dying animal or a man in a fit. There was no trace of compassion in their blank faces, no glint of curiosity in their dull gaze. In their complete detachment they seemed devoid of the instincts of human humanity.

"Where am I?" she asked wildly.

A woman in a black overall suddenly broke into guttural speech, which conveyed no iota of meaning to Iris. She listened with the same helpless panic which had shaken her yesterday in the gorge. Actually the woman's face was so close that she could see the pits in her skin and the hairs sprouting inside her nostrils; yet their fundamental cleavage was so complete that they might have been standing on different planets.

She wanted some one to lighten her darkness—to raise the veil which baffled her and blinded her. *Something* had happened to her of which she had no knowledge.

Her need was beyond the scope of crude pantomime. Only some lucid explanation could clear the confusion of her senses. In that moment she thought of the people at the hotel, from whom she had practically run away. Now she felt she would give years of her life to see the strong saintly face of the clergyman looking down at her, or meet the kind eyes of his wife.

In an effort to grip reality she looked around her. The place was vaguely familiar, with dark wooden walls and a sanded floor, which served as a communal spittoon. A bar of dusty sunlight, slanting through a narrow window, glinted on thick glasses stacked upon a shelf and on a sheaf of fluttering handbills.

She raised her head higher and felt a throb of dull pain, followed by a rush of dizziness. For a moment she thought she was going to be sick; but the next second nausea was overpowered by a shock of memory.

This was the waiting-room at the station. She had lingered here only yesterday, with the crowd, as it gulped down a final drink. Like jolting trucks banging through her brain her thoughts were linked together by the connecting sequence of the railway. She remembered sitting on the platform, in the sunshine, while she waited for a train.

Her heart began to knock violently. She was on her way back to England. Yet she had not the least idea as to what had happened after her black-out, or how long ago it had occurred. The express might have come—and gone—leaving her behind.

In her overwrought state the idea seemed the ultimate catastrophe. Her head swam again and she had to

44

wait for a mist to clear from her eyes before she could read the figures on her tiny wrist watch.

To her joy she discovered that she had still twenty-five minutes in which to pull herself together before her journey.

"What happened to me?" she wondered. "What made me pass out? Was I attacked?"

Closing her eyes, she tried desperately to clear her brain. But her last conscious moment held only a memory of blue sky and grass-green lake, viewed as though through a crystal.

Suddenly she remembered her bag and groped to find it. To her dismay it was not beside her, nor could she see it anywhere on the bench. Her suitcase lay on the floor, and her hat had been placed on top of it, as though to prove the limit of her possessions.

"My bag," she screamed, wild-eyed with panic. "Where's my bag?"

It held not only her money and tickets, but her passport. Without it, it was impossible for her to continue her journey. Even if she boarded the train, penniless, she would be turned back at the first frontier.

The thought drove her frantic. She felt sure that these staring women had combined to rob her when she was helpless and at their mercy. When she sprang from the bench they pulled her down again.

The blood rushed to her head and she resisted them fiercely. As she struggled she was conscious of a whirl of confusion—of throbbing pain, rising voices, and lights flashing before her eyes. There were breathless panting noises, as an undercurrent to a strange rushing sound, as though an imprisoned fountain had suddenly burst through the ground.

In spite of her efforts, the woman in the black pinafore dragged her down again, while a fat girl, in a bursting bodice, held a glass to her lips. When she refused to swallow they treated her like a child, tilting her chin and pouring the spirit down her throat.

It made her cough and gasp, until her head seemed to be swelling with pain. Terrified by this threat of another attack, she relaxed in helpless misery. Her instinct warned her that, if she grew excited, at any moment the walls might rock—like the snow-mountains—as a prelude to total extinction.

Next time she might not wake up. Besides, she dared not risk being ill in the village, alone, and so far away from her friends. If she returned to the hotel she could enlist the financial help of the English visitors, while, doubtless, another passport could be procured; but it meant delay.

In addition, these people were all strangers to her, whose holiday was nearly ended. In another day they would be gone, while she might be stranded there, indefinitely, exposed to indifference, and even neglect. The hotel, too, was closing down almost immediately.

"I mustn't be ill," thought Iris. "I must get away at once while there is still time."

She felt sure that, if she could board the train, the mere knowledge that she was rolling, mile by mile, back to civilisation, would brace her to hold out until she reached some familiar place. She thought of Basle on the milky-jade Rhine, with its excellent hotels where English

46

was spoken and where she could be ill, intelligibly, and with dignity.

Everything hung upon the catching of this train. The issue at stake made her suddenly desperate to find her bag. She was struggling to rise again, when she became conscious that some one was trying to establish contact with her.

It was an old man in a dirty blouse, with a gnarled elfin face—brown and lined as the scar on a tree-trunk, from which a branch has been lopped. He kept taking off his greasy hat and pointing, first upwards, and then to her head.

All at once she grasped his meaning. He was telling her that while she sat on the platform she had been attacked with sunstroke.

The explanation was a great relief, because she was both frightened and baffled by the mystery of her illness. She rarely ailed and had never fainted before. Besides, it had given her proof that in spite of her own misgiving, the channels were not entirely blocked, provided the issues were not too involved.

Although she still felt sick with anxiety about her train, she managed to smile faintly at the porter. As though he had been waiting for some sign of encouragement, he thrust his hand into the neck of his dirty blouse and drew out her bag.

With a cry, she snatched it from him. Remembering the crowd on the platform, she had no hope of finding her money; but there was a faint chance that her passport had not been stolen.

She tore at the zip-fastener with shaking fingers, to

find, to her utter amazement, that the contents were intact. Tickets, money, passport—even her receipted hotel-bill—were still there.

She had grossly maligned the native honesty, and she hastened to make amends. Here, at last, was a situation she understood. As usual, some one had come to her rescue, true to the tradition of the protective square in her palm. Her part, which was merely to overpay for services rendered, was easy.

The women received their share of the windfall with stolid faces. Apparently they were too stunned with astonishment to show excitement or gratitude. The old porter, on the other hand, beamed triumphantly and gripped Iris' suitcase, to show that he, too, had grasped the situation.

In spite of her resistance to it, the raw spirit, together with her change of circumstance, had revived Iris considerably. She felt practically restored again and mistress of herself as she showed her ticket to the porter.

The effect on him was electric. He yammered with excitement, as he grabbed her arm and rushed with her to the door. Directly they had passed through it, Iris understood the origin of the curious pervading noise which had helped to complicate her nightmare.

It was the gush of steam escaping from an engine. While she had let the precious minutes slip by, the express had entered the station.

Now it was on the point of departure.

The platform was a scene of wild confusion. Doors were being slammed. People were shouting farewells and crowding before the carriages. An official waved a flag and the whistle shrilled.

They were one minute too late. Iris realised the fact that she was beaten, just as, the porter—metaphorically—snatched at the psychological moment, and was swung away with it on its flight. He took advantage of the brief interval between the first jerk of the engine and the revolution of the wheels, to charge the crowd, like an aged tiger. There was still strength and agility in his sinewy old frame to enable him to reach the nearest carriage and wrench open the door.

His entrance was disputed by a majestic lady in black. She was a personage to whom—as a peasant—his bones instinctively cringed. On the other hand, his patron had paid him a sum far in excess of what he earned in tips during the whole of a brief season.

Therefore, his patron must have her place. Ducking under the august lady's arm, he hurled Iris' suitcase into the compartment and dragged her inside after it.

The carriage was moving when he scrambled out, to fall in a heap on the platform. He was unhurt, however, for when she looked back to wave her thanks, he grinned at her like a toothless gnome.

Already he was yards behind. The station slid by, and the lake began to lap against the piles of the rough landing-stage. It rippled past the window in a sheet of emerald, ruffled by the breeze and burnished by the sun. As the train swung round the curve of the rails to the cutting in the rocks, Iris looked back for a last view of the village—a fantastic huddle of coloured toy-buildings, perched on the green shelf of the valley.

CHAPTER VII

PASSENGERS

As the train rattled out of the cliff tunnel and emerged in a green tree-choked gorge, Iris glanced at her watch. According to the evidence of its hands, the Trieste express was not yet due at the village station.

"It must have stopped when I crashed," she decided. "Sweet luck. It might have lost me my train."

The reminder made her feel profoundly grateful to be actually on her way back to England. During the past twenty-four hours she had experienced more conflicting emotions than in a lifetime of easy circumstance and arrangement. She had known the terrifying helplessness of being friendless, sick, and penniless—with every wire cut. And then, at the worst, her luck had turned, as it always did.

From force of contrast the everyday business of transport was turned into a temporary rapture. Railway travel was no longer an infliction, only to be endured by the aid of such palliatives as reservations, flowers, fruit, chocolates, light literature, and a group of friends to shriek encouragement.

As she sat, jammed in an uncomfortable carriage, in a train which was not too clean, with little prospect of securing a wagon-lit at Trieste, she felt the thrill of a first journey.

The scenery preserved its barbarous character in rugged magnificence. The train threaded its way past piled-up chunks of disrupted landscape, like a Doré steel-engraving of Dante's Inferno. Waterfalls slashed the walls of granite precipices with silver-veining. Sometimes they passed arid patches, where dark pools, fringed with black-feathered rushes, lay in desolate hollows.

Iris gazed at it through the screen of the window—glad of the protective pane of glass. This grandeur was the wreckage of a world shattered by elemental force, and reminded her that she had just been bruised by her first contact with reality.

She still shrank from the memory of first facts, even although the nightmare railway station was the thick of the mountain away. Now that it was slipping farther behind the coils of the rails with every passing minute, she could dare to estimate the narrow margin by which she had escaped disaster.

Amid the crowd at the station there must have been a percentage of dishonest characters, ready to take advantage of the providential combination of an unconscious foreigner—who did not count—and an expensive handbag which promised a rich loot. Yet the little gnome-like porter chanced to be the man on the spot.

"Things always do turn out for me," she thought. "But—it must be appalling for some of the others."

It was the first time she had realised the fate of those unfortunates who had no squares in their palms. If there were a railway accident, she knew that she would be in the unwrecked middle portion of the train, just as inevitably as certain other passengers were doomed to be in the telescoped coaches.

As she shuddered at the thought, she glanced idly at

the woman who sat opposite to her. She was a negative type in every respect—middle-aged, with a huddle of small indefinite features, and vague colouring. Some one drew a face and then rubbed it nearly out again. Her curly hair was faded and her skin was bleached to oatmeal.

She was not sufficiently a caricature to suggest a stage spinster. Even her tweed suit and matching hat were not too dowdy, although lacking any distinctive note.

In ordinary circumstances, Iris would not have spared her a second glance or thought. To-day, however, she gazed at her with compassion.

"If *she* were in a jam, no one would help her out," she thought.

It was discomforting to reflect that the population of the globe must include a percentage of persons without friends, money, or influence; nonentities who would never be missed, and who would sink without leaving a bubble.

To distract her thoughts, Iris tried to look at the scenery again. But the window was now blocked by passengers who were unable to find seats, so stood in the corridor. For the first time, therefore, she made a deliberate survey of the other occupants of her compartment.

They were six in number—the proper quota—which she had increased to an illegal seven. Her side was occupied by a family party—two large parents and one small daughter of about twelve.

The father had a shaven head, a little waxed moustache, and several chins. His horn-rimmed glasses and comfortable air gave him the appearance of a prosperous citizen. His wife had an oiled straight black fringe, and bushy eyebrows which looked as though they had been corked. The child wore babyish socks, which did not match her adult expression. Her hair had apparently been set, after a permanent wave, for it was still secured with clips.

They all wore new and fashionable suits, which might have been inspired by a shorthand manual. The father wore stripes—the mother, spots—and the daughter, checks. Iris reflected idly that if they were broken up, and reassembled, in the general scramble, they might convey a message to the world in shorthand.

On the evidence, it would be a motto for the home, for they displayed a united spirit, as they shared a newspaper. The mother scanned the fashions; the little girl read the children's page; and from the closely-printed columns Iris guessed that the head of the family studied finance.

She looked away from them to the opposite side of the carriage. Sitting beside the tweed spinster was a fair pretty girl, who appeared to have modelled herself from the photograph of any blonde film actress. There were the same sleek waves of hair, the large blue eyes—with supplemented lashes, and the butterfly brows. Her cheeks were tinted and her lips painted to geranium bows.

In spite of the delicacy of her features, her beauty was lifeless and standardised. She wore a tight white suit, with a high black satin blouse, while her cap, gauntlet-gloves and bag were also black. She sat erect and motionless, holding a rigid pose, as though she were being photographed for a "still."

Although her figure was reduced almost to starvation-point, she encroached on the tweed spinster's corner, in order to leave a respectful gap between herself and the personage who had opposed Iris' entrance.

There was no doubt that this majestic lady belonged to the ruling classes. Her bagged eyes were fierce with pride, and her nose was an arrogant beak. Dressed and semi-veiled in heavy black, her enormous bulk occupied nearly half the seat.

To Iris' astonishment, she was regarding her with a fixed stare of hostility. It made her feel both guilty and self-conscious.

"I know I crashed the carriage," she thought. "But *she's* got plenty of room. Wish I could explain, for my own satisfaction."

Leaning forward, she spoke impulsively to the personage.

"Do you speak English?"

Apparently the question was an insult, for the lady closed her heavy lids with studied insolence, as though she could not endure a plebeian spectacle.

Iris bit her lip as she glanced at the other passengers. The family party kept their eyes fixed on their paper—the tweed spinster smoothed her skirt, the blonde beauty stared into space. Somehow, Iris received an impression that this well-bred unconsciousness was a tribute of respect to the personage.

"Is she the local equivalent of the sacred black bull?" she wondered angrily. "Can't anyone speak until she

54

does? . . . Well, to *me*, she's nothing but a fat woman with horrible kid gloves."

She tried to hold on to her critical attitude, but in vain. An overpowering atmosphere of authority seemed to filtrate from the towering black figure.

Now that her excitement was wearing off, she began to feel the after-effects of her slight sunstroke. Her head ached and the back of her neck felt as stiff as though it had been reinforced by an iron rod. The symptoms warned her to be careful. With the threat of illness still hanging over her, she knew she should store up every scrap of nervous force, and not waste her reserves in fanciful dislikes.

Her resolution did not save her from increasing discomfort. The carriage seemed not only stuffy, but oppressive with the black widow's personality. Iris felt positive that she was a clotted mass of prejudices—an obstruction in the healthy life-stream of the community. Her type was always a clog on progress.

As her face grew damp, she looked towards the closed windows of the compartment. The corridor-end, where she sat, was too crowded to admit any of the outer air, so she struggled to her feet and caught the other strap.

"Do you mind?" she asked with stressed courtesy, hoping, from her intonation, that the other passengers would grasp the fact that she was asking their permission before letting down the glass.

As she expected, the man of the family party rose and took the strap from her. Instead of finishing the job, however, he glanced respectfully at the personage, as though she were sacrosanct, and then frowned at Iris, shaking his head the while.

Feeling furious at the opposition, Iris returned to her corner.

"I've got to take it," she thought. "Take it on the chin. I'm the outsider here."

It was another novel sensation for the most popular member of the crowd, to be in a minority. Besides having to endure the lack of ventilation, the inability to explain her actions, or express a wish, gave her the stunted sense of being deprived of two faculties—speech and hearing.

Presently the door was opened and a tall man squeezed into the carriage. Although she realised that her feelings had grown super-sensitive, Iris thought she had never seen a more repulsive face. He was pallid as potter's clay, with dead dark eyes, and a black spade beard.

He bowed to the personage and began to talk to her, standing the while. His story was evidently interesting, for Iris noticed that the other passengers, including the child, were all listening with close interest.

As he was speaking, his glasses flashed round the compartment, and finally rested on her. His glance was penetrating, yet impersonal, as though she were a specimen on a microscope-slide. Yet, somehow, she received the impression that she was not a welcome specimen, nor one that he had expected to see.

Stooping so that his lips were on a level with the personage's ear, he asked a low-toned question. She replied in a whisper, so that Iris was reminded of two blowflies buzzing in a bottle.

"Am I imagining things, or do these people really dislike me?" she wondered.

She knew that she was growing obsessed by this impression of a general and secret hostility. It was manifestly absurd, especially as the man with the black spade beard had not seen her before. She had merely inconvenienced some strangers, from whom she was divided by the barrier of language.

Shutting her eyes, she tried to forget the people in the carriage. Yet the presence of the man continued to affect her with discomfort. His white face seemed to break through her closed lids, and float in the air before her.

It was a great relief when the buzzing ceased and she heard him go out of the compartment. Directly he had left, she grew normal again, and was chiefly conscious of a very bad headache. The most important things in life were tea and cigarettes; yet she dared not smoke because of the threat of sickness, while tea seemed a feature of a lost civilisation.

The train was now rushing through a deserted country of rock and pine. The nearest reminder of habitation was an occasional castle of great antiquity, and usually in ruins. As she was gazing out at the fantastic scenery, an official poked his head in at the door and shouted something which sounded like blasphemy.

The other passengers listened in apathy, but Iris began to open her bag, in case tickets or passport were required. As she did so, she was amazed to hear a crisp English voice.

The tweed spinster had risen from her seat and was asking her a question.

"Are you coming to the restaurant-car to get tea?"

CHAPTER VIII

TEA-INTERVAL

Iris was too stunned with surprise to reply. She looked incredulously at the sandy, spiney stretches, flowing past the window, as though expecting to see them turn to Swiss chalets, or blue Italian lakes.

"Oh," she gasped, "you're English."

"Of course. I thought I looked typical. . . . Are you coming to tea?"

"Oh, *yes*."

As Iris followed her guide out of the carriage, she was rather disconcerted to find that their compartment was at the end of the corridor. It looked as though her protective square had not insured her against railway smashes, after all.

"Are we next to the engine?" she asked.

"Oh, no," the tweed lady assured her. "There are ordinary coaches in between. It's an extra long train, because of the end of the season rush. They had to pack them in with a shoe-horn."

Apparently she was the type that collected information, for she began to broadcast almost immediately.

"Just glance at the next carriage to ours as you go by—and I'll tell you something."

Although Iris felt no curiosity, she obeyed. Afterwards, she was sorry, because she could not forget what she saw.

A rigid figure, covered with rugs, lay stretched on the

length of one seat. It was impossible to tell whether it were a man or a woman, for head, eyes and forehead were bandaged, and the features concealed by a criss-cross of plaster strips. Apparently the face had been gashed to mutilation-point.

Iris recoiled in horror, which was increased when she realised that the pallid man with the spade beard was in charge of the invalid. Beside him was a nun, whose expression was so callous that it was difficult to connect her with any act of mercy.

While they chatted together, the patient feebly raised one hand. Although they saw the movement, they ignored it. They might have been porters, responsible for the transport of a bit of lumber, instead of a suffering human being.

The fluttering fingers affected Iris with a rush of acute sympathy. She shrank from the thought that—had the cards fallen otherwise—she, too, might be lying, neglected by some indifferent stranger.

"That nun looks a criminal," she whispered.

"She's not a nun," the tweed lady informed her, "she's a nursing-sister."

"Then I pity her patient. Ghastly to be ill on a journey. And she's not a spectacle. Why can't they pull down the blind?"

"It would be dull for them."

"Poor devil. I suppose it's a man?"

Iris was so foolishly anxious to break the parallel between the motionless figure and herself, that she was disappointed when her companion shook her head.

"No, a woman. They got in at our station, higher up.

The doctor was telling the Baroness about it. She's just been terribly injured in a motor smash, and there's risk of serious brain injury. So the doctor's rushing her to Trieste, for a tricky operation. It's a desperate chance to save her reason and her life."

"Is that man with the black beard a doctor?" asked Iris.

"Yes. Very clever, too."

"Is he? I'd rather have a vet."

The tweed lady, who was leading, did not hear her muttered protest. They had to force their way through the blocked corridors, and had covered about half the distance when the spinster collided with a tall dark lady in grey, who was standing at the door of a crowded carriage.

"Oh, I'm so sorry," she apologised. "I was just looking out to see if our tea was coming. I gave the order to an attendant."

Iris recognised Mrs. Barnes' voice, and shrank back, for she was not anxious to meet the vicar and his wife.

But her companion gave a cry of delight.

"Oh, you're English, too," she said. "This is my lucky day."

As Mrs. Barnes' soft brown eyes seemed to invite confidence, she added, "I've been in exile for a year."

"Are you on your way home?" asked Mrs. Barnes, with ready sympathy.

"Yes, but I can't believe it. It's far too good to be true. Shall I send a waiter with your tea?"

"That would be really kind. My husband is such a wretched traveller. Like so many big strong men."

Iris listened impatiently, for her temples were beginning to throb savagely. Now that Mrs. Barnes had managed to introduce her husband's name into the conversation, she knew that her own tea might be held up indefinitely.

"Aren't we blocking the way?" she asked.

Mrs. Barnes recognised her with rather a forced smile, for the Gabriel episode still rankled.

"Surprised to see us?" she asked. "We decided, after all, not to wait for the last through train. And our friends—the Miss Flood-Porters, came with us. In fact, we're a full muster, for the honeymooners are here, too."

Iris had struggled a little farther down the surging corridor, when the tweed lady spoke to her over her shoulder.

"What a sweet face your friend has! Like a suffering madonna."

"Oh, no, she's very bright," Iris assured her. "And she's definitely not a friend."

They crossed the last dangerously clanking connecting-way, and entered the restaurant-car, which seemed full already. The Misses Flood-Porter—both wearing well-cut, white linen travelling-coats—had secured a table and were drinking tea. Their formal bow, when Iris squeezed by them, was conditional recognition before the final fade-out.

"We'll speak to you during the journey," it seemed to say, "but at Victoria we become strangers."

As Iris showed no inclination to join them, Miss Rose could not resist the temptation to manage a situation.

"Your friend is trying to attract your attention," she called out.

Iris turned and saw that her companion had discovered the last spare corner—a table wedged against the wall—and was reserving a place for herself. When she joined her, the little lady was looking round her with shining eyes.

"I ordered the tea for your nice friends," she said. "Oh, isn't all this *fun*?"

Her pleasure was so spontaneous and genuine that Iris could not condemn it as gush. She stared doubtfully at the faded old-gold plush window-curtains, the smutty tablecloth, the glass dish of cherry jam—and then she glanced at her companion.

She received a vague impression of a little puckered face; but there was a sparkle in the faded blue eyes, and an eager note in the voice, which suggested a girl.

Afterwards, when she was trying to collect evidence of what she believed must be an extraordinary conspiracy, it was this discrepancy between a youthful voice and a middle-aged spinster which made her doubt her own senses. In any case, her recollection was far from clear, for she did not remember looking consciously at her companion again.

The sun was blazing in through the window, so that she shaded her eyes with one hand most of the time she was having tea. But as she listened to the flow of excited chatter, she had the feeling that she was being entertained by some one much younger than herself.

"Why do you like it?" she asked.

"Because it's travel. We're moving. Everything's moving."

Iris also had the impression that the whole scene was flickering like an early motion-picture. The waiters swung down the rocking carriage, balancing trays. Scraps of country flew past the window. Smuts rained down on the flakes of butter and the sticky cakes. Dusty motes quivered in the rays of the sun, and the china shook with every jerk of the engine.

As she tried to drink some tea before it was all shaken over the rim of her cup, she learned that her companion was an English governess—Miss Winifred Froy—and was on her way home for a holiday. It came as a shock of surprise to know that this adult lady actually possessed living parents.

"Pater and Mater say they can talk of nothing else but my return," declared Miss Froy. "They're as excited as children. And so is Sock."

"Sock?" repeated Iris.

"Yes, short for Socrates. The Pater's name for him. He is our dog. He's an Old English sheep-dog—not pure—but *so* appealing. And he's really devoted to me. Mater says he understands that I'm coming home, but not *when*. So the old duffer meets every train. And then the darling comes back, with his tail down, the picture of depression. Pater and Mater are looking forward to seeing his frantic joy the night I *do* come."

"I'd love to see him," murmured Iris.

The old parents' happiness left her unmoved, but she was specially fond of dogs. She got a clear picture of Sock—a shaggy mongrel—absurdly clownish and overgrown, with amber eyes beaming under his wisps, and gambolling like a puppy in the joy of reunion.

Suddenly, Miss Froy broke off, at a recollection.

"Before I forget I want to explain why I did not back you up about the window. No wonder you thought I could not be English. It was *stuffy*—but I didn't like to interfere, because of the Baroness."

"D'you mean the appalling black person?"

"Yes, the Baroness. I'm under an obligation to her. There was a muddle about my place in the train. I'd booked second-class, but there wasn't a seat left. So the Baroness most kindly paid the difference, so that I could travel first-class, in her carriage."

"Yet she doesn't look kind," murmured Iris.

"Perhaps she is rather overwhelming. But she's a member of the family to which I had the honour of being governess. . . . It's not wise to mention names in public, but I was governess to the very highest in the place. These remote districts are still feudal, and centuries behind us. You can have no idea of the *power* of the—of my late employer. What he says *goes*. And he hasn't got to speak. A nod is enough."

"Degrading," muttered Iris, who resented authority.

"It is," agreed Miss Froy. "But it's in the atmosphere, and after a time one absorbs it and one grows spineless. And that's not English. . . . I feel so reinforced, now I've met you. We must stick together."

Iris made no promise. Her fright had not changed her fundamentally, only weakened her nerve. She had the modern prejudice in favour of youth, and had no intention of being tied to a middle-aged spinster for the rest of the journey.

"Are you going back again?" she asked distantly.

"Yes, but not to the castle. It's rather awkward, but I wanted another twelve months to perfect my accent, so I engaged to teach the children of the—well, we'll call him the leader of the opposition."

She lowered her voice to a whisper.

"The truth is, there is a small but growing Communist element, which is very opposed to my late employer. In fact, they've accused him of corruption and all sorts of horrors. I don't ask myself if it's true, for it's not my business. I only know he's a marvellous man, with wonderful charm and personality. Blood tells. . . . Shall I tell you something rather indiscreet?"

Iris nodded wearily. She was beginning to feel dazed by the heat and incessant clatter. Her tea had not refreshed her, for most of it had splashed into her saucer. The engine plunged and jolted over the metals with drunken jerks, belching out wreaths of acrid smoke which streamed past the windows.

Miss Froy continued her serial, while Iris listened in bored resignation.

"I was terribly anxious to say good-bye to the—to my employer, so that I could assure him that my going over to the enemy—so to speak—was not treachery. His valet and secretary both told me that he was away at his hunting-lodge. But somehow I felt that they were putting me off. Anyway, I lay awake until early morning, before it was light, when I heard water splashing in the bathroom. . . . Only one, my dear, for the castle arrangements were primitive, although my bedroom was like a stage royal apartment, all gilding and peacock-blue velvet, with a huge circular mirror let into the ceiling. . . . Well, I crept out, like a mouse, and met him in the corridor. There we were, plain man and woman—I in my dressing-gown, and he in his bath-robe, and with his hair all wet and rough. . . . But he was charming. He actually shook my hand and thanked me for my services."

Miss Froy stopped to butter the last scrap of roll. As she was wiping her sticky fingers, she heaved a sigh of happiness.

"I cannot tell you," she said, "what a relief it was to leave under such pleasant circumstances. I always try to be on good terms with every one. Of course, I'm insignificant, but I can say truthfully that I have not got an enemy in the world."

CHAPTER IX

COMPATRIOTS

"AND now," said Miss Froy, "I suppose we had better go back to our carriage, and make room for others."

The waiter, who was both a judge of character and an opportunist, presented the bill to Iris. Unable to decipher the sprawling numerals, she laid down a note and rose from her seat.

"Aren't you waiting for your change?" asked Miss Froy.

When Iris explained that she was leaving it for a tip, she gasped.

"But it's absurb. Besides, they've already charged their percentage on the bill. . . . As I'm more familiar with the currency, hadn't I better settle up for everything? I'll keep an account, and we can get straight at our journey's end."

The incident was fresh evidence of the smooth working of the protective-square system. Although Iris was travelling alone, a competent courier had presented herself, to rid her of all responsibilities and worries.

"She's decent, although she's a crashing bore," she decided, as she followed Miss Froy down the swaying restaurant-car.

She noticed that the Misses Flood-Porter, who had not finished their leisurely tea, took no notice of herself, but looked exclusively at her companion.

Miss Froy returned Miss Rose's stare with frank interest.

"Those people are English," she whispered to Iris, not knowing that they had met before. "They're part of an England that is passing away. Well-bred privileged people, who live in big houses, and don't spend their income. I'm rather sorry they're dying out."

"Why?" asked Iris.

"Because, although I'm a worker myself, I feel that nice leisured people stand for much that is good. Tradition, charity, national prestige. They may not think you're their equal, but their sense of justice sees that you get equal rights."

Iris said nothing, although she admitted to herself that, while they were at the hotel, the Misses Flood-Porter were more considerate of person and property than her own friends.

When they made their long and shaky pilgrimage through the train, she was amazed by Miss Froy's youthful spirits. Her laugh rang out whenever she was bumped against other passengers, or was forced, by a lurch of the engine, to clutch a rail.

After they had pushed their way to a clearer passage, she lingered to peep through the windows of the reserved compartments. One of these specially arrested her attention and she invited Iris to share her view.

"Do have a peek," she urged. "There's a glorious couple, just like film stars come to life."

Iris was feeling too jaded to be interested in anything but a railway collision; but as she squeezed her way past

Miss Froy, she glanced mechanically through the glass, and recognised the bridal pair from the hotel.

Even within the limits of the narrow coupé, the Todhunters had managed to suggest their special atmosphere of opulence and exclusion. The bride wore the kind of elaborate travelling-costume which is worn only on journeys inside a film studio, and had assembled a drift of luxurious possessions.

"Fancy," thrilled Miss Froy, "they've got hot-house fruit with their tea. Grapes and nectarines. . . . He's looking at her with his soul in his eyes, but I can only see her profile. It's just like a beautiful statue. Oh, lady, please turn your head."

Her wish was granted, for, at that moment, Mrs. Todhunter chanced to glance towards the window. She frowned when she saw Miss Froy and spoke to her husband, who rose instantly and pulled down the blind.

Although she was not implicated, Iris felt ashamed of the incident; but Miss Froy only bubbled with amusement.

"He'll know me again," she said. "He looked at me as if he'd like to annihilate me. Quite natural. I was the World—and he wants to forget the World, because he's in paradise. It must be wonderful to be exclusively in love."

"They may not be married," remarked Iris. "Anyone can buy a wedding-ring."

"You mean—guilty love? Oh, no, they're too glorious. What name did they register under?"

"Todhunter."

"Then they *are* married. I'm so glad. If it was an

70

irregular affair, they would have signed 'Brown', or 'Smith.' It's always done."

As she listened to the gush of words behind her, Iris was again perplexed, by the discrepancy between Miss Froy's personality and her appearance. It was as though a dryad were imprisoned within the tree-trunk of a withered spinster.

When they reached the end of the corridor, a morbid impulse made her glance towards the carriage which held the invalid. She caught a glimpse of a rigid form and a face hidden by its mass of adhesions, before she looked quickly away, to avoid the eyes of the doctor.

They frightened her, because of their suggestion of baleful hypnotic force. She knew that they would be powerless to affect her in ordinary circumstances; but she was beginning to feel heady and unreal, as though she were in a dream, where every emotion is intensified.

In all probability this condition was a consequent symptom of her sunstroke, and was due, partly, to her struggle to hold out, until she could collapse safely at her journey's end. She was directing her will-power towards one aim only, and therefore draining herself of energy.

As a result she was susceptible to imaginary antagonism. When she caught sight of a blur of faces inside the gloom of her carriage, she shrank back, unwilling to enter.

She received unexpected support from Miss Froy, who seemed to divine her reluctance.

"Don't let's sit mum like charity-children any longer," she whispered. "Even if I *am* under an obligation to the

71

Baroness, I am going to remember that these people are only foreigners. They shan't impress me. *We're* English."

Although the reminder was patriotism reduced to its lowest term of Jingoism, it braced Iris to enter the compartment with a touch of her old abandon. Precaution forgotten, she lit a cigarette without a glance at the other passengers.

"Have you travelled much?" she asked Miss Froy.

"Only in Europe," was the regretful reply. "Mater doesn't really like me going so far from home, but she holds the theory that the younger generation must not be denied their freedom. Still, I've promised to stick to Europe, although, whenever I'm near a boundary, I just ache to hop over the line to Asia."

"Is your mother very old?"

"No, she's eighty years young. A real sport, with the spirit of the modern girl. Pater is seventy-seven. He never let her know he was younger than she, but it leaked out when he had to retire at sixty-five. Poor Mater was terribly upset. She said, 'You have made me feel a cradle-snatcher.' . . . Oh, I can't believe I'm really going to see them again soon."

As she listened, Iris watched the smoke curling up from her cigarette. Occasionally she saw a vague little puckered face swaying amid the haze, like an unsuccessful attempt at television. Out of gratitude for services rendered—and still to come—she tried to appreciate the old parents, but she grew very bored by the family saga.

She learned that Pater was tall and thin, and looked classical, while Mater was short and stout, but dignified.

Apparently Pater had unquenchable ardour and energy, for at the age of seventy he began to learn Hebrew.

"He's made a detailed time-table for every month of his life, up to ninety," explained Miss Froy. "That's what comes of being a schoolmaster. Now, Mater is passionately fond of novels. Love ones, you know. She makes a long bus journey every week to change her library book. But she says she can't imagine them properly unless she makes *me* the heroine."

"I'm sure you had a marvellous time," said Iris.

Miss Froy resented the attempt to be tactful.

"Have, and had," she declared. "Pater was a parson before he kept a school, and his curates always proposed to me. I expect it is because I have fair curly hair. . . . And I still have the excitement and hope of the eternal quest. I never forget that a little boy is born for every little girl. And even if we haven't met yet, we are both growing old together, and if we're fated to meet, we *shall*."

Iris thought sceptically of the mature men who refuse to adhere to the calendar, as she listened with rising resentment. She wanted quiet—but Miss Froy's voice went on and on, like the unreeling of an endless talking-picture.

Presently, however, Miss Froy recaptured her interest, for she began to talk of languages.

"I speak ten, including English," she said. "At first, when you're in a strange country, you can't understand one word, and you feel like a puppy thrown into a pond. You flounder and struggle, so unless you want to drown you've simply got to pick it up. By the end of a year you're as fluent as a native. But I always insist on staying a second year, for the sake of idiomatic polish."

"*I* expect foreigners to speak English," declared Iris.

"When you're off the map they may not, and then you might find yourself in a terrible fix. Shall I tell you a true story?"

Without waiting for encouragement, Miss Froy span a yarn which was not calculated to cool Iris' inflamed nerves. It was all very vague and anonymous, but the actual horror was stark.

A certain woman had been certified as insane, but owing to a blunder the ambulance went to the wrong house and forcibly took away an Englishwoman, who did not understand a word of the language, or of her destination. In her indignation and horror at finding herself in a private asylum, she became so vehement and violent that she was kept, at first, under the influence of drugs.

When the mistake was found out, the doctor—who was a most unscrupulous character—was afraid to admit it. At the time he was in financial difficulties, and he feared it might ruin his reputation. So he planned to detain the Englishwoman until he could release her as officially cured.

"But she couldn't know she wasn't in for life," explained Miss Froy, working up the agony. "The horror of it would probably have driven her really insane, only a nurse exposed the doctor's plot, out of revenge. . . . But can you imagine the awful position of that poor English-woman? Trapped, with no one to make inquiries about her, or even to know she had disappeared, for she was

74

merely a friendless foreigner, staying a night here, and a night there, at some pension. She didn't understand a word—she couldn't explain—"

"Please *stop*," broke in Iris. "I can imagine it all. Vividly. But would you mind if we stopped talking?"

"Oh, certainly. Aren't you well? It's difficult to be sure, with your sunburn, but I thought you looked green, once or twice."

"I'm very fit, thanks. But my head aches a bit. I've just had a touch of sunstroke."

"Sunstroke? When?"

Knowing that Miss Froy's curiosity had to be appeased, Iris gave a brief account of her attack. As she did so, she glanced round the carriage. It was evident, from the blank faces, that—with one exception—the passengers did not understand English.

Iris could not be certain about the Baroness. She had the slightly stupid expression of an autocrat who has acquired power through birth, and not enterprise; yet there was a gleam of intelligence in her eyes that betrayed secret interest in the story.

"Oh, you poor soul," cried Miss Froy, who overflowed with sympathy. "Why didn't you stop me chattering before? I'll give you some aspirin."

Although she hated any fuss, it was a relief to Iris when she was able to sit back in her corner, while Miss Froy hunted among the contents of her bag.

"I don't think you had better have dinner in the restaurant-car," she decided. "I'll bring you something here, later. Now, swallow these tablets, and then try to get a little nap."

After Iris had closed her eyes, she could still hear Miss Froy fluttering about her, like a fussy little bird, on guard. It gave her a curious sense of protection, while the carriage was so warm that she soon became pleasantly drowsy.

As the drug began to take effect, her thoughts grew jumbled, while her head kept jerking forward. Presently she lost consciousness of place, as she felt herself moving onwards with the motion of the train, as though she were riding. Sometimes she took a fence, when the seat seemed to leap under her, leaving her suspended in the air.

Clankety-clankety-*clank*. On and on. She kept moving steadily upwards. Clankety-clankety-*clank*. Then the rhythm of the train changed, and she seemed to be sliding backwards down a long slope. Click-click-click-click. The wheels rattled over the rails, with a sound of castanets.

She was sinking deeper and deeper, while the carriage vibrated like the throbbing of an airplane. It was bearing her away—sweeping her outside the carriage—to the edge of a drop. . . .

With a violent start she opened her eyes. Her heart was leaping, as though she had actually fallen from a height. At first she wondered where she was; then as she gradually recognised her surroundings, she found that she was staring at the Baroness.

In slight confusion she looked away quickly to the opposite seat.

To her surprise, Miss Froy's place was empty.

CHAPTER X

THE VACANT SEAT

Iris was ungratefully glad of Miss Froy's absence. Her doze had confused rather than refreshed her, and she felt she could not endure another long instalment of family history. She wanted peace; and while it was impossible to have quiet, amid the roar and rush of the train, she considered herself entitled, at least, to personal privacy.

As regarded the other passengers, she was free from any risk of contact. Not one of them took the slightest notice of her. The Baroness slept in her corner—the others sat motionless and silent. Inside the carriage, the atmosphere was warm and airless as a conservatory.

It soothed Iris to a tranquil torpidity. She felt numbed to thought and feeling, as though she were in a semi-trance and incapable of raising a finger, or framing two consecutive words. Patches of green scenery fluttered past the window, like a flock of emerald birds. The Baroness' heavy breathing rose and fell with the regularity of a tide.

Iris vaguely dreaded Miss Froy's return, which must destroy the narcotic spell. At any moment, now, she might hear the brisk step in the corridor. Presumably Miss Froy had gone to wash, and had been obliged to wait her turn, owing to the crowd.

Hoping for the best, Iris closed her eyes again. At first she was apprehensive whenever any one passed by the window, but each false alarm increased her sense of security. Miss Froy ceased to be a menace and shrank to a mere name. The octogenarian parents went back to their rightful place inside some old photograph-album. Even Sock—that shaggy absurd mongrel, whom Iris had grown to like—was blurred to an appealing memory.

Clankety-clankety-*clank*. The sound of breathing swelled to the surge of a heavy sea, sucking at the rocks. Muted by the thunder of the train, it boomed in unison with the throb of the engine. Clankety-clankety-*clank*.

Suddenly the Baroness' snores arose to an elephantine trumpet which jerked Iris awake. She started up in her seat—tense with apprehension and with every faculty keyed up. The shock had vibrated some seventh sense which made her expectant of disaster, as she glanced swiftly at Miss Froy's place.

It was still empty.

She was surprised by her pang of disappointment. Not long ago she had been praying for Miss Froy's return to be delayed; but now she felt lonely and eager to welcome her.

"I expect I'll soon be cursing her again," she admitted to herself. "But, anyway, she is human."

She glanced at the blonde beauty, who was beginning to remind her of a wax model in a shop window. Not a flat wave of her honey-gold hair was out of place. Even her eyes had the transparency of blue wax.

Chilled by the contrast to the vital little spinster, Iris looked at her watch. The late hour, which told her that she had slept longer than she had suspected, also made her feel rather worried about Miss Froy's prolonged absence.

"She's had enough time to take a bath," she thought. "I—I hope nothing's wrong."

The idea was so disturbing that she exerted all her common sense to dislodge it.

"Absurd," she told herself. "What *could* happen to her? It's not night, when she might open the wrong door by mistake, and step out of the train in the dark. Besides, she's an experienced traveller—not a helpless fool like myself. And she knows about a hundred languages."

A smile flickered over her lips as she remembered one of the little spinster's confidences.

"Languages give me a sense of power. If an international crisis arose in a railway carriage, and there were no interpreters, I could step into the breach and, perhaps, alter the destinies of the world."

The recollection suggested an explanation for Miss Froy's untenanted seat. Probably she was indulging her social instincts by talking to congenial strangers. She was not divided from them by any barrier of language. Moreover, she was in holiday mood and wanted to tell every one that she was going home.

"I'll give her another half-hour," decided Iris. "She *must* be back by then."

As she looked out of the window, the clouded sky on late afternoon filled her with melancholy. The train had been gradually descending from the heights, and was now steaming through a lush green valley. Mauve crocuses cropped up amid thick pastures, which were darkened by moisture. The scene was definitely autumnal and made her realise that summer was over.

The time slipped away too quickly, because she dreaded reaching the limit which she had appointed. If Miss Froy did not return she would have to make a decision, and she did not know what to do. Of course, as she reminded herself, it was not really her business at all; but her uneasiness grew with the passing of each five minutes of grace.

Presently there was a stir among the other passengers. The little girl began to whine fretfully, while the father appeared to reason with her. Iris guessed that she had complained of sleepiness, and had been persuaded to take a nap, when she saw the mother's preparations to keep her daughter's trim appearance intact.

After the black patent belt and the organdie collar had been removed, she drew out a net and arranged it carefully over the little girl's permanent wave. The blonde beauty showed her first signs of animation as she watched the process, but her interest died when the matron pulled off her child's buckled shoes and replaced them with a pair of shabby bedroom-slippers.

Finally she pointed to Miss Froy's vacant place.

Iris felt a rush of disproportionate resentment when she saw the little girl sitting in the spinster's seat. She wished she could protest by signs, but was too self-conscious to risk making an exhibition of herself.

"When she comes back, Miss Froy will soon turn her out," she thought.

Upon reflection, however, she was not so sure of direct action. When she remembered the friendly spirit

Miss Froy displayed towards every one, she felt certain that she had already established a pleasant understanding with her fellow passengers.

The little girl was so heavy with sleep that she closed her eyes directly she curled up in her corner. The parents looked at each other and smiled. They caught the blonde beauty's attention, and she, too, nodded with polite appreciation. Only Iris remained outside the circle.

She knew that she was unjustly prejudiced, since she was the real interloper, yet she hated this calm appropriation of Miss Froy's place. It was as though the other passengers were taking unfair advantage of her absence —since she could not turn out a sleeping child.

Or even as though they were acting on some secret intelligence.

They were behaving as though they *knew* she was not coming back. In a panic, Iris looked at her watch, to find, to her dismay, that the half-hour had slipped away.

The lapse of time was registered outside the window. The overcast sky had grown darker and the first mists were beginning to collect in the corners of the green saturated fields. Instead of crocuses, she saw the pallid fungoid growths of toadstools or mushrooms.

As the sadness of twilight stole over her, Iris began to hunger for company. She wanted cheerful voices, lights, laughter; but although she thought wistfully of the crowd, she was even more anxious to see a little lined face and hear the high rushing voice.

Now that she was gone, she seemed indefinite as a

dream. Iris could not reconstruct any clear picture of her, or understand why she should leave such a blank.

"What was she *like*?" she wondered.

At that moment she chanced to look up at the rack. To her surprise, Miss Froy's suitcase was no longer there.

In spite of logic, her nerves began to flutter at this new development. While she told herself that it was obvious that Miss Froy had moved to another compartment, the circumstances did not fit in. To begin with, the train was so overcrowded that it would be difficult to find an empty unreserved place.

On the other hand, Miss Froy had mentioned some muddle about her seat. It was barely possible that it had proved available, after all.

"No," decided Iris, "the Baroness had already paid the difference for her to travel first. And I'm sure she wouldn't leave me without a word of explanation. She talked of bringing me dinner. Besides, I owe her for my tea. I'm simply bound to find her."

She looked at the other passengers, who might hold the key to the mystery. Too distracted now to care about appearances, she made an effort to communicate with them. Feeling that "English" was the word which should have lightened their darkness, she started in German.

"Wo ist die Dame *English*?"

They shook their heads and shrugged, to show that they did not understand. So she made a second attempt.

"Où est la dame *English*?"

As no sign of intelligence dawned on their faces, she spoke to them in her own language.

"Where is the English lady?"

The effort was hopeless. She could not reach them, and they showed no wish to touch her. As they stared at her, she was chilled by their indifference, as though she were outside the pale of civilised obligations.

Feeling suddenly desperate, she pointed to Miss Froy's seat, and then arched her brows in exaggerated inquiry. This time she succeeded in arousing an emotion, for the man and his wife exchanged amused glances, while the blonde's lip curled with disdain. Then, as though she scented entertainment, the little girl opened her black eyes and broke into a snigger, which she suppressed instantly at a warning glance from her father.

Stung by their ridicule, Iris glared at them, as she crossed to the Baroness and shook her arm.

"Wake up, please," she entreated.

She heard a smothered gasp from the other passengers, as though she had committed some act of sacrilege. But she was too overwrought to remember to apologise, when the Baroness raised her lids and stared at her with outraged majesty.

"Where is Miss Froy?" asked Iris.

"Miss Froy?" repeated the Baroness. "I do not know anyone who has that name."

Iris pointed to the seat which was occupied by the little girl.

"She sat *there*," she said.

The Baroness shook her head.

"You make a mistake," she declared. "No English lady has sat there ever."

Iris' head began to reel.

"But she *did*," she insisted. "I talked to her. And we went and had tea together. You must remember."

"There is nothing to remember." The Baroness spoke with slow emphasis. "I do not understand what you mean at all. I tell you this. . . . There has been no English lady, here, in this carriage, never, at any time, except you. *You* are the only English lady here."

CHAPTER XI

NEEDLE IN A HAYSTACK

Iris opened her lips only to close them again. She had the helpless feeling of being shouted down by some terrific blast of sound. The Baroness had made a statement which was an outrage on the evidence of her senses; but it was backed up by the force of an overpowering authority.

As she held the girl's eye, challenging her denial, Iris looked at the leaden eyelids, the deep lines graven from nose to chin—the heavy obstinate chin. The lips were drawn down in a grimace which reminded her of a mask of the Muse of Tragedy.

She realised that further protest was useless. The Baroness would flatten down any attempt at opposition with relentless pressure. The most she could do was to acknowledge defeat with a shrug which disdained further argument.

Her composure was only bluff for she felt utterly bewildered as she sank back in her seat. She was scarcely conscious of slides of twilight scenery streaming past the window, or of the other passengers. A village shot out of the shadows and vanished again in the dimness. She caught the flash of a huddle of dark roofs and the white streak of a little river, which boiled under a hooded bridge.

The next second the church tower and wooden houses were left behind as the express rocked on its way

85

back to England. It lurched and shrieked as though in unison with the tangle of Iris' thoughts.

"No Miss Froy? Absurd. The woman must be mad. Does she take me for a fool?. . . But why does she say it? *Why*?"

It was this lack of motive which worried her most. Miss Froy was such a harmless little soul that there could be no reason for her suppression. She was on friendly terms with every one.

Yet the fact remained that she had disappeared, for Iris was positive now that she would not come back to the carriage. In a sudden fit of nerves she sprang to her feet.

"She must be somewhere on the train," she argued. "I'll find her."

She would not admit it, but her own confidence was flawed by the difficulty of finding a reason for Miss Froy's absence. She had taken Iris under her wing, so that it was entirely out of line with her character as a kindly little busybody for her to withdraw in such an abrupt and final manner.

"Does she think I might be sickening for some infectious disease?" she wondered. "After all, she's so terribly keen to get back to her old parents and the dog, that she wouldn't dare run risks of being held up. Naturally she would sacrifice me."

Her progress down the train was a most unpleasant experience. It had been difficult when Miss Froy acted the part of a fussy little tug and had cleared a passage for her. Now that more passengers had grown tired of sitting in cramped compartments and had emerged to stretch, or smoke, the corridor was as closely packed with tourists as a melon with seeds.

Iris did not know how to ask them to step aside and she did not like to push. Moreover, the fact that she was attractive did not escape the notice of some of the men. Each time a swerve of the express caused her to lurch against some susceptible stranger, he usually believed that she was making overtures.

Although she grew hot with annoyance her chief emotion was one of futility. She had no hope of finding Miss Froy in such confusion. Whenever she passed each fresh compartment to peer inside she always saw the same blur of faces.

Because she was beginning to run a temperature, these faces appeared as bleared and distorted as creations of a nightmare. It was a relief when she worked her way down the train, in an unavailing search, to see the vicar and his wife in one of the crowded carriages.

They were sitting opposite to each other. Mr. Barnes had closed his eyes and his face was set. In spite of his sunburn it was plain that he was far from well and was exerting his will-power to subdue his symptoms.

His wife watched him with strained attention. She looked wan and miserable, as though—in imagination—she was sharing his every pang of train-sickness.

She did not smile when Iris struggled inside and spoke to her.

"Sorry to bother you but I'm looking for my friend."

"Oh, yes?"

There was the familiar forced brightness in Mrs. Barnes' voice but her eyes were tragic.

"You remember her?" prompted Iris. "She sent the waiter with your tea."

The vicar came to life.

"It was kind indeed," he said. "Will you give her my special thanks?"

"When I find her," promised Iris. "She went out of the carriage some time ago—and she hasn't come back."

"I haven't noticed her pass the window," said Mrs. Barnes. "Perhaps she went to wash. Anyway, she couldn't possibly be lost."

Iris could see that she was concentrating on her husband and had no interest in some unknown woman.

"Can I find her for you?" offered the vicar manfully, struggling to his feet.

"Certainly *not*." His wife's voice was sharp. "Don't be absurd, Kenneth. You don't know what she looks like."

"That's true. I should be more hindrance than help."

The vicar sank back gratefully and looked up at Iris with a forced smile.

"Isn't it humiliating to be such a wretched traveller?" he asked.

"I wouldn't talk," advised his wife.

Iris took the hint and went out of the compartment. She, too, considered the vicar's weakness was a major misfortune. He was not only a man of high principle but she was sure that he possessed imagination and sympathy; yet she was unable to appeal to him for help because nature had laid him low.

Because she was beginning to fear that she faced failure she grew more frantic with determination to find

Miss Froy. If she failed she was loaded with a heavy responsibility.

Of all the people in the train she—alone—seemed conscious of the disappearance of a missing passenger.

She shrank from the prospect of trying to arouse these callous strangers from their apathy. As she clung to rails and was buffeted by the impacts of other tourists pushing their way past her, she hated them all. In her strung-up condition she could not realise that these people might experience her own sensations were they suddenly placed in a crowded London Tube or New York Subway and jostled by seemingly hostile and indifferent strangers.

When she reached the reserved portion of the train, the blind was still pulled down over the Todhunters' window, but she recognised the Misses Flood-Porter in one of the reserved coupés. They sat on different sides of the tiny compartment—each with her feet stretched out on the seat. The elder lady wore horn-rimmed glasses and was reading a Tauchnitz, while Miss Rose smoked a cigarette.

They looked very content with life and although kind-hearted, the sight of others standing in the corridors subtly enhanced their appreciation of their own comfort.

"Smug," thought Iris bitterly.

They made her realise her own position. She reminded herself that her place, too, was in a reserved compartment, instead of fighting her way into the privacy of strange people.

"Why am I taking it?" she wondered as she met the unfriendly glance of the ladies. Miss Rose's was perceptibly more frigid as though she were practising gradations, in preparation for the cut direct at Victoria Station.

At last she had combed the train with the exception of the restaurant-car. Now that tea was finished it was invaded by men who wanted to drink and smoke in comfort.

As she lingered at the entrance to make sure that Miss Froy was not inside seeking her soul-mate of whom she had spoken, a hopeful young man touched Iris' arm. He said something unintelligible which she translated as an invitation to refreshment, and leered into her face.

Furious at the liberty she shook him off and was on the point of turning away, when, amid the rumble of masculine voices, she distinguished the distinctive vowels of an Oxford accent.

She was trying to locate it when she caught sight of the spade-bearded doctor. His bald, domed head, seen through the murk of smoke, reminded her of a moon rising through the mist. His face was blanched and bony—his dead eyes were magnified by his thick glasses.

As they picked her out with an impersonal gaze, she felt as though she had been pinned down and classified as a type.

Suddenly—for no reason at all—she thought of the doctor in Miss Froy's tale of horror.

CHAPTER XII

WITNESSES

Although she was conscious of the interest she aroused, Iris was too overwrought to care. Raising her voice she made a general appeal.

"Please. Is there anyone English here?"

The spectacle of a pretty girl in distress made a young man leap to his feet. He was of rather untidy appearance with a pleasant ordinary face and audacious hazel eyes.

"Can I be of use?" he asked quickly.

The voice was familiar to Iris. She had heard it at the railway station, just before her sunstroke. This was the young man who had been opposed to trial by jury. He looked exactly as she had pictured him; he had even a rebellious tuft of hair, of the kind that lies down under treatment, as meekly as a trained hound, but which springs up again, immediately the brush is put away.

In other circumstances she would have been attracted to him instinctively; but in this crisis he seemed to lack ballast.

"Gets fresh with barmaids and cheeks traffic-cops," she reflected swiftly.

"Well?" prompted the young man.

To her dismay Iris found it difficult to control her voice or collect her thoughts when she tried to explain the situation.

"It's all rather complicated," she said shakily. "I'm in a jam. At least, it's nothing to do with me. But I'm sure there's some horrible mistake and I can't speak a word of this miserable language."

"That's all right," said the young man encouragingly. "I speak the lingo. Just put me wise to the trouble."

While Iris still hesitated, doubtful of her choice of champion, a tall, thin man rose reluctantly from his seat, as though chivalry were a painful duty. In this case his academic appearance was not misleading, for directly he spoke Iris recognised the characteristic voice of the professor of modern languages.

"May I offer my services as an interpreter?" he asked formally.

"He's no good," broke in the young man. "He only knows grammar. But I can swear in the vernacular and we may need a spot of profanity."

Iris checked her laugh, for she realised that she was on the verge of hysteria.

"An Englishwoman has disappeared from the train," she told the Professor. "She's a *real* person, but the Baroness says—"

Her voice suddenly failed as she noticed that the doctor was looking at her with fixed attention. The Professor's glacial eye also reminded her that she was making an exhibition of herself.

"Could you pull yourself together to make a coherent statement?" he asked.

The chill in his voice was tonic, for it braced her to compress the actual situation into a few words. This time she was careful to make no allusion to the Baroness but confined herself to Miss Froy's non-return to the carriage.

To her relief the Professor appeared to be impressed, for he rubbed his long chin gravely.

"You said—an *English* lady?" he asked.

"Yes," replied Iris eagerly. "Miss Froy. She's a governess."

"Ah, yes. . . . Now, are you absolutely certain that she is nowhere on the train?"

"Positive. I've looked everywhere."

"H'm. She would not be likely to leave her reserved seat for an inadequate reason. At what time precisely did she leave the compartment?"

"I don't know. I was asleep. When I woke up she wasn't there."

"Then the first step is to interview the other passengers. If the lady does not return by that time, I may consider calling the guard and asking for an official examination of the train."

The young man winked at Iris, to direct her attention to the fact that the Professor was in his element.

"Gaudy chance for you to rub up the lingo, Professor," he said.

The remark reminded Iris that while the Professor's acquaintance with the language would be academic, the young man probably possessed a more colloquial knowledge. This was important, since she was beginning to think that the confusion over Miss Froy sprang from the Baroness' imperfect command of English. Her accent was good, but if she could not understand all that was said she would never admit ignorance.

Determined to leave nothing to chance, Iris appealed to the frivolous youth.

"Will you come, too, and swear for us?" she asked.

"Like a bird," he replied. "A parrot, I mean, of course. Lead on, Professor."

Iris' spirits rose as they made their way back through the train. Although she was still worried about Miss Froy, her companion infused her with a sense of comradeship.

"My name's Hare," he told her. "Much too long for you to remember. Better call me Maximilian—or, if you prefer it, Max. What's yours?"

"Iris Carr."

"Mrs.?"

"Miss."

"Good. I'm an engineer out here. I'm building a dam up in some mountains."

"What fun! I'm nothing."

Full of confidence in the support of her compatriots, Iris felt exultant as they neared her carriage. Tourists—seated on their suitcases—blocked the way and children chased each other, regardless of adult toes. As a pioneer Hare was better than Miss Froy. While she hooted to warn others of their approach, he rammed a clear passage, like an ice-plough.

The Professor stood aside to allow Iris to enter the compartment first. She noticed immediately that the spade-bearded doctor was seated beside the Baroness and was talking to her in low rapid tones. He must have left the restaurant-car in a hurry.

The fact made her feel slightly uneasy.

"He's one jump ahead of me," she thought.

The family party shared a bag of nectarines and took no notice of her, while the blonde was absorbed in

94

rebuilding the curves of her geranium lips. The Baroness sat unmoved as a huge black granite statue.

There was a glint in Iris' eyes when she made her announcement.

"Two English gentlemen have come to make some inquiries about Miss Froy."

The Baroness reared up her head and glared at her, but made no comment. It was impossible to tell whether the announcement were a shock.

"Will you kindly allow me to enter?" asked the Professor.

In order to make more room for the investigation, Iris went out into the corridor. From where she stood she could see the invalid's carriage and the nursing-sister who sat at the window. In spite of her pre-occupation, she noticed that the woman's face was not repulsive but merely stolid.

"Am I exaggerating everything?" she wondered nervously. "Perhaps, after all, I'm *not* reliable."

In spite of her pity for the wretched patient it was a real relief when the original nurse, with the callous expression, appeared at the door. The fog of mystery, together with the throb of her temples, combined to make her feel uncertain of herself.

She smiled when Hare spoke to her.

"I'm going to listen-in," he told her. "The Professor's bound to be a don at theory, but he might slip up in practice, so I'll check up for you."

Iris looked over his shoulder as she tried to follow the proceedings. The Professor seemed to carry out his investigation with thoroughness, patience and personal dignity. Although he bowed to the Baroness with respect, before he explained the situation, he conveyed an impression of his own importance.

The personage inclined her head and then appeared to address a general question to her fellow-passengers. Iris noticed how her proud gaze swept each face and that her voice had a ring of authority.

Following her lead the Professor interrogated every person in turn—only to receive the inevitable shake of the head, which appeared the language of the country. Remembering her own experience Iris whispered to Hare.

"Can't they understand him?"

He replied by a nod which told her that he was listening closely and did not wish to be disturbed. Thrown on her own resources she made her own notes and was amused to remark that—in spite of being accustomed to teach mixed classes—the Professor was scared of the ladies, including the little girl.

Very soon he confined his questions to the businessman, who answered with slow deliberation. He was obviously trying to be helpful to a foreigner, who might have difficulty in understanding him. In the end he produced his card and gave it to the Professor, who read it, and then returned it with a bow of thanks.

In spite of the general atmosphere of politeness Iris grew impatient and tugged Hare's arm.

"Is he finding out anything about Miss Froy?" she asked.

She was unpleasantly surprised by his grave face.

"Oh, it's rather involved," he told her. "All about where is the pen of the aunt of my gardener!"

Her confidence began to cloud as she grew conscious of an unfriendly atmosphere. The Baroness did not remove her eyes from her face during her short speech, to which the Professor listened with marked respect. At its end she made a sign to the doctor, as though ordering him to support her statement.

Hitherto he had been a silent witness of the scene. His white impassive face and dead eyes made him resemble one newly-returned from the grave, to attend a repeat performance of the revue of life—to its eternal damnation.

But as he began to talk at his patron's bidding he grew vital and even vehement, for he used his hands to emphasise his words.

When he had finished speaking the Professor turned to Iris.

"You appear to have made an extraordinary mistake," he said. "No one in this carriage knows anything about the lady you *say* is missing."

Iris stared at him incredulously.

"Are you telling me I invented her?" she asked angrily.

"I hardly know what to think."

"Then I'll tell you. All these people are telling lies."

Even as she spoke Iris realised the absurdity of her charge. It was altogether too wholesale. No rational person could believe that the passengers would unite to bear false witness. The family party in particular looked solid and respectable, while the father was probably the equivalent to her own lawyer.

The Professor was of the same opinion, for his manner grew stiffer.

"The people whom you accuse of being liars are citizens of good standing," he said, "and are known personally to the Baroness, who vouches for their integrity. The gentleman is not only a well-known banker in the district, but is also the Baroness' banker. The young lady"—he glanced warily at the blonde—"is the daughter of her agent."

"I can't help that," protested Iris. "All I know is that I'm owing Miss Froy for my tea. She paid for me."

"We can check up on that," interrupted Hare. "If she paid, you'll be so much to the good. Just count up your loose cash."

Iris shook her head.

"I don't know how much I had," she confessed. "I'm hopeless about money. I'm always getting R.D. cheques."

Although the Professor's mouth turned down at the admission, he intervened in proof of his sense of fair play.

"If you had tea together," he said, "the waiter should remember your companion. I'll interview him next, if you will give me a description of the lady."

Iris had been dreading this moment because of her clouded recollection of Miss Froy. She knew that she had barely glanced at her the whole time they were together. During tea she had been half-blinded by the sun, and when they returned to the carriage she had kept her eyes closed on account of her headache. On their way to and from the restaurant-car, she had always been either in front or behind her companion.

"I can't tell you much," she faltered. "You see, there's nothing much about her to catch hold of. She's middle-aged, and ordinary—and rather colourless."

"Tall or short? Fat or thin? Fair or dark?" prompted Hare.

"Medium. But she said she had fair curly hair."

"'Said'?" repeated the Professor. "Didn't you notice it for yourself?"

"No. But I think it looked faded. I remember she had blue eyes, though."

"Not very enlightening, I'm afraid," remarked the Professor.

"What did she wear?" asked Hare suddenly.

"Tweed. Oatmeal, flecked with brown. Swagger coat, finger-length, with patch pockets and stitched cuffs and scarf. The ends of the scarf were fastened with small blue-bone buttons and she wore a natural tussore shirt-blouse, stitched with blue—a different shade—with a small blue handkerchief in the breast-pocket. I'm afraid I didn't notice details much. Her hat was made of the same material, with a stitched brim and a Récamier crown, with a funny bright-blue feather stuck through the band."

"Stop," commanded Hare. "Now that you've remembered the hat, can't you make another effort and put a face under it?"

He was so delighted with the result of his experiment that his dejection was ludicrous when Iris shook her head in the old provoking manner.

"No, I can't remember any face. You see, I had such a frantic headache."

"Exactly," commented the Professor dryly. "Cause and effect, I'm afraid. The doctor has been telling us that you had a slight sunstroke."

As though awaiting his cue the doctor—who had been listening intently—spoke to Iris.

"That blow of the sun explains all," he said, speaking in English, with slow emphasis. "It has given you a delirium. You saw some one who is not there. Afterwards, you went to sleep, and you dream. Then, presently, you awake and you are much better. So you saw Miss Froy no more. . . . She is nothing but a delirium—a dream."

CHAPTER XIII

A DREAM WITHIN A DREAM

At first Iris was too surprised to protest. She had the bewildered sensation of being the one sane person in a mad world. Her astonishment turned to indignation when the Professor caught Hare's eye and gave a nod of mutual understanding.

Then he spoke to Iris in a formal voice.

"I think we may accept that as final. If I had known the circumstances I should not have intervened. I hope you will soon feel better."

"We'd better clear and let Miss Carr get some quiet," suggested Hare, with a doubtful grin.

Iris felt as though she were being smothered with feather-bed opposition. Controlling her anger she forced herself to speak calmly.

"I'm afraid it's not so simple as that. As far as I'm concerned the matter's by no means ended. Why should you imagine I'm telling a lie?"

"I do not," the Professor assured her. "I am convinced it is your mistake. But, since you've raised the point of fairness, you must admit that the weight of evidence is against you. I have to be fair. . . . Can *you* explain why six persons should lie?"

Iris had a sudden flash of intuition.

"I can't," she said, "unless one person started the lie, and the others are backing her up. In that case it's only her word against mine. And as I'm English and you're

English and this concerns an Englishwoman, it's your duty to believe *me*."

As she spoke Iris challenged the Baroness in an accusing stare. Although the personage heard the charge with complete composure, the Professor coughed in protest.

"You mustn't confuse patriotism with prejudice," he said. "Besides, your insinuation is absurd. What motive would the Baroness have for telling a lie?"

Iris' brain began to swim.

"I don't know," she said weakly. "It's all such a mystery. No one could want to injure Miss Froy. She's too insignificant. Besides, she was proud of having no enemies. And she told me herself that the Baroness had been kind."

"What have I done?" asked the Baroness blandly.

"She said that there was a muddle about her place and you paid the excess-fare for her to travel in here."

"That was charming of me. I'm gratified to hear of my generosity. Unfortunately I know nothing of it. But the ticket-collector should be able to refresh my memory."

The Professor turned to Iris dutifully.

"What am I to do?" he asked. "You are making things rather difficult by persisting in this attitude. But, if you insist, I will question the man."

"I'll dig him out," offered Hare.

Iris knew that he wanted a chance to escape. She felt that his sympathies were with her while he withheld his faith.

After he had gone the Professor began to talk to the Baroness and the doctor, presumably for the sake of further practice. Suspicious of every glance and inflection, Iris believed that he was explaining the delicacy of his position and stressing the absurdity of the charge, for the Baroness looked almost as benevolent as a sated tigress that kills just for the sport.

She was glad when Hare—his rebellious tuft sticking out like a feather—battled his way down the corridor, followed by the ticket-collector. He was a sturdy young man in a very tight uniform and he reminded Iris of a toy soldier, with two blobs of damson-colour on his broad cheeks and a tiny black waxed moustache.

As he entered the Baroness spoke to him sharply and then waved to the Professor to continue.

By this time Iris' nerve was shattered; she was so sure that the ticket-collector would prove another victim to mass-hypnotism that she was prepared when Hare made a grimace. "He's telling the old, old story," he said.

"Of course he is." Iris tried to laugh. "I expect he was one of her peasants. He looks bucolic. She seems to own the lot—including you and the Professor."

"Now, don't get het up," he urged. "I know just what you are feeling. I've been through this myself. I'll tell you about it, if I can dislodge this young lady."

The little girl, who had been making precocious eyes at Hare, responded to his invitation to move with shrugs and pouts of protest. All the same she reluctantly went back to her original place, while he squeezed into the corner originally occupied by the elusive spinster.

"Cheer up," he said. "Unless your Miss Froy was invisible, other people in the train must have seen her."

"I know," nodded Iris. "But I can't think. My brain's too sticky."

The Professor, who was just leaving the compartment, caught the drift of Hare's argument, for he turned back to speak to Iris. "If you can produce some definite proof of this lady's existence, I'm still open to conviction. But I sincerely hope that you will not expose us and yourself to further ridicule."

Iris felt too limp for defiance. "Thank you," she said meekly. "Where shall I find you?"

"In the reserved portion."

"We're sharing a bunny-hutch," supplemented Hare. "Didn't you know we're rich? We started a prosperity chain."

"I hate that man," burst out Iris when the Professor had gone.

"Oh, no," protested Hare, "he's not a bad old fossil. You've got him scared stiff because you're young and attractive."

Then the grin faded from his lips.

"I want to bore you with a true story," he said. "Some years ago, I was playing in an international at Twickenham. Just before the match both teams were presented to the Prince of Wales and he shook hands with all of us. Well, after I'd scored the winning try—I had to slip that in—I got kicked on the head in a scrum and passed out. Later on, when I was fairly comfortable in a private ward at the hospital, the nurse came in, all of a flutter, and said there was a special visitor to see me."

"The Prince?" asked Iris, trying to force an intelligent interest.

"The same. Of course, he didn't stay more than a minute. Just smiled at me and said he hoped I'd soon be all right and he was sorry about my accident. I was so steamed up I thought I wouldn't sleep a wink, but I dropped off the instant he had gone. Next morning the nurses said, 'Weren't you pleased to see your captain?'"

"Captain?"

"Yes, the captain of the team. It was definitely *not* the Prince. . . . And yet I saw him as plainly as I see you. He shook hands with me and said something nice about my try. He was *real*. And that's what a spot of head trouble can do to the best of us."

Iris set her lips obstinately.

"I thought you believed in me," she said. "But you're like the rest. Please go away."

"I will, because I'm sure you ought to keep quiet. Try and get some sleep."

"No. I've got to think this out. If I let myself believe all of you, I should be afraid I was getting mental. And I'm not. I'm *not*."

"Now take it easy."

"What a soothing nurse you'd make! You only want a silly cap. Listen." Iris dropped her voice. "I'm extra in the dark, because I couldn't understand these questions. Do you really *know* the language?"

"Better than English now. And it was so elementary that even the Professor couldn't slip up. Sorry—but there are no holes anywhere. . . . But you look all in. Let me get you a life-saver."

"No. Miss Froy promised she'd get me something and I prefer to wait for her."

Her defiant eyes told Hare that she was nailing her colours to the mast. Since he regarded Miss Froy as a kind of ghost, he did not think that Iris would derive benefit from anything she might bring, so he resolved to renew his offer later. Meanwhile he could serve her best by leaving her alone.

Just as he was going he remembered something and beckoned Iris into the corridor.

"There was just one bit I didn't tumble to," he confessed. "The Baroness spoke to the ticket chap in a dialect which was Chinese to me."

"Then that proves they came from the same district," cried Iris triumphantly.

"Hum. But as we don't know what she said it's not too helpful. Salaams. See you later."

After Hare had gone Iris crouched in her corner, rocking with the vibration of the train. It was clattering through a succession of short tunnels and the air was full of sound, as though a giant roller were flattening out the sky. The noise worried her acutely. She had scarcely eaten all day and was beginning to feel exhausted. But although she was unused to being ill, and was consequently frightened, she was far more alarmed by the jangling of her brain.

She started violently when a nursing-sister appeared in the doorway and beckoned to the doctor. She hardly noticed the relief of his absence, because her thoughts raced in a confused circle round the central incident of the black-out.

"I was on the platform, one second—and the next second I went out. Where did I go? Was the waking up in the waiting-room, and all those women, and the funny little old porter—*real*? Of course they were, or I should not be on the train. . . . But I met Miss Froy *afterwards*. They say she's only my dream. So, if she's a dream, it means that I've dreamed the waiting-room and the train and that I'm not on the train at all. I'm not awake yet. . . . If it was true, it would be enough to drive anyone mad."

She resolutely fought back the rising tide of hysteria.

"But it's absurd. I *am* awake and I'm here in this train. So I *did* meet Miss Froy. . . . Only I'm up against some mystery and I have to fight a pack of lies. All right, then, I *will*."

At this stage her concern was for herself, rather than for Miss Froy. She had been spoiled since her birth, so it was natural for her to be selfish; and because that self was a gay and charming entity, the world had united to keep her fixed at her special angle.

But now her ego was getting involved with the fate of an obscure and unattractive spinster. Once again she began to review the incidents of their meeting. And then, suddenly, her clouded brain cleared and a sealed cell in her memory became unblocked.

The Baroness looked at her as she sprang from her seat.

"Is madame worse?" she asked.

"Better, thanks," replied Iris. "And I'm going to test some English memories, just for a change. I'm going to talk to some English visitors from my hotel who saw me with Miss Froy."

CHAPTER XIV

FRESH EVIDENCE

Now that she was about to establish Miss Froy's existence, Iris began to wonder what had become of her.
When she remembered her exhaustive search of the
train it seemed positive that she could not be there. But
it was also impossible for her to be anywhere else.

The corridors and carriages were thronged with tourists, so that she could not open a door or window to
jump out, without attracting immediate attention. It was
equally certain that no one could make a parcel of her
and dump her on the permanent way, without becoming
an object of general interest.

There was no place for her to hide—nor could Iris
conceive any motive for such a course. In short, she was
protected from any form of injury—accidental or inten-
tional—by the presence of a cloud of witnesses.

In despair Iris shelved the problem.

"She can't be proved missing until it's proved that she
was there in the first place," she argued. "That's my job.
After that, the others must carry on."

As she remembered the Professor's standard for reliable evidence she felt she could understand a show-man's
pride in his exhibits. Her witnesses must satisfy the most
exacting taste—being British to the core.

The Baroness looked at her when she opened her bag
and drew out her pocket-mirror and lipstick. Although
her detachment was complete and her face void of

expression, she somehow conveyed an impression of secret activity, as though she were spinning mental threads.

"She's pitting her brain against mine," thought Iris, in a sudden flurry. "I must get in first."

Directly she began to hurry she went to pieces again. Her hands shook so that she painted her mouth with a streak of vivid red—more suggestive of crushed fruit than the crimson blossom after which the tint was named. Unable to find her comb she gave up the attempt and dashed out into the corridor.

Men stared at her and women muttered complaints as she pushed them aside without apology. As a matter of fact she was hardly conscious of them, except as so many obstacles in her way. After so much delay, every wasted moment was a personal reproach. In her excitement she could only see—a long way off—the blurred figure of a little spinster. She must hurry to reach it. But faces kept coming in between her and her goal—faces that grinned or scowled—the faces of strangers. They melted away like a mist, only to give place to other faces. There was a flash of eyes and teeth—a jam of bodies. She thrust and struggled, while her cheeks burned and a wave of hair fell across her cheeks.

When at last she won through to the clearer stretch of corridor, the sight of the Professor—smoking, while he looked through the window—reminded her of the conventions. She felt ashamed of her haste and she spoke breathlessly.

"Do I look like a jigsaw? It was that devastating crowd. They wouldn't let me through."

The Professor did not smile, for in spite of a pictur-esque attraction her wild hair and brilliant colour produced a wanton effect which did not appeal to him. Neither did Mr. Todhunter approve her, as he criticised her through the open door of his coupé.

Although he claimed to be a judge of feminine charm, he was of the type that prefers a lily-pond to a waterfall. He never lingered before an unframed picture, for he exacted the correct setting for beauty. Abandon was only permissible in a negligée and definitely bad form on a train journey. Although he had often seen Iris, when she looked like a member of an undress beauty chorus, he had never noticed her until the evening when she wore a becoming frock.

"Who's the girl?" asked the bride as she flicked over the pages of a pictorial paper.

He lowered his voice. "One of the mob from the hotel."

"Help."

In the next coupé Miss Rose Flood-Porter raised her head from the soft leather cushion without which she never travelled. Her movement roused her sister from her doze, and she, too, strained to listen.

Unconscious of her audience Iris spoke to the Profes-sor in a high excited voice.

"Your marvellous witnesses have let you down. They were all telling lies. The six of them."

He looked at her burning cheeks with cold concern.

"Is your head worse?" he asked.

"Thanks, I'm perfectly fit. . . . And I can prove Miss Froy was with me, because the English visitors from my hotel saw her, too. We'll get in touch with the English Consul when we reach Trieste and he'll hold up the train for a thorough examination. Oh, you'll see."

Iris thrilled at the prospect of her triumph. At that moment she seemed to see the Union Jack fluttering overhead and hear the strains of the National Anthem.

The Professor smiled with dreary patience.

"I'm waiting to be convinced," he reminded her.

"Then you shall be." Iris swung round to find herself facing Mr. Todhunter. "You'll help me find Miss Froy, won't you?" she asked confidently.

He smiled down indulgently at her but he did not reply at once. It was the pause of deliberation and was characteristic of his profession.

"I shall be delighted to co-operate with you," he told her. "But—who *is* Miss Froy?"

"An English governess who is missing from the train. You must remember her. She peeped in at your window and you jumped up and drew down the blind."

"That is exactly what I should have done in the circumstances. Only, in this case, the special circumstance did not arise. No lady did me the honour to linger by my window."

His words were so unexpected that Iris caught her breath, as though she were falling through space.

"Didn't you *see* her?" she gasped.

"No."

"But your wife called your attention to her. You were both annoyed."

The beautiful Mrs. Todhunter, who had been listening, broke in with none of her habitual languor. "We are not a peep-show and no one looked in. . . . Do you mind if we shut the door? I want to rest before dinner."

The Professor turned to Iris with forced kindness.

"You're tired," he said. "Let me take you back to your carriage."

"No." Iris shook off his hand. "I won't let the matter rest. There are others. These ladies—"

Dashing into the next coupé where the Misses Flood-Porter now sat upright in dignity, she appealed to them.

"You'll help me find Miss Froy, won't you? She's *English*."

"May I explain?" interposed the Professor as the ladies looked to him for enlightenment.

Iris could hardly control her impatience as she listened to the cultured drawl. Her eyes were fixed on the solid fresh-coloured faces of the sisters. Then Miss Rose spoke.

"I have no recollection of your companion. Some one may have been with you, but I was not wearing my glasses."

"Neither was I," remarked Miss Flood-Porter. "So you can understand that we shall not be able to help you. It would be against our principles to identify some one of whom we were not sure."

"Most unfair," commented Miss Rose. "So, please, don't refer to us. If you do, we must refuse to interfere."

Iris could hardly believe her ears.

"But isn't it against your principles not to raise a finger to help an Englishwoman who may be in danger?" she asked hotly.

"Danger?" echoed Miss Rose derisively. "What could

happen to her on a crowded train? Besides, there are plenty of other people who are probably more observant than ourselves. After all, there is no reason why we should be penalised because we are English."

Iris was too bewildered by the unexpected collapse of her hopes, to speak. She felt that she had been betrayed by her compatriots. They might boast of wearing evening dress for the honour of their country, but they had let down England. The Union Jack lay shredded in tatters and the triumphant strains of the National Anthem died down to the screech of a tin whistle.

She hated them all so fiercely that when the vicar's wife put her head round the door she could only glare at her.

Mrs. Barnes gave a general smile as she explained her presence.

"My husband is sleeping now, so I thought I'd run in for a chat. When we travel, I'm first in command, which is a new experience for me and only comes once a year."

She spoke eagerly as though to justify her husband's weakness. Then she turned to Iris, who was following the Professor from the coupé.

"Don't let me drive you away."

"Nothing could keep me." Iris spoke with bitter hopelessness. "Of course, *you* didn't see Miss Froy?"

"Was that the little lady in tweed, with a blue feather in her hat?" asked Mrs. Barnes. "Why, *of course*, I remember her, and her kindness. We were so grateful for the tea."

CHAPTER XV

TRANSFORMATION SCENE

Her relief was so overwhelming that Iris felt on the verge of tears as she turned to the Professor.

"Are you convinced now?" she asked shakily.

The Professor glanced at the vicar's wife with almost an apologetic air, for the lady was a familiar type which he admired and approved, when it was safely married to some one else.

"The question is unnecessary," he said. "It was simply a matter of getting corroborative evidence. I'm sorry to have doubted your word in the first place. It was due to the unfortunate circumstance of your sunstroke."

"Well, what are you going to do?" insisted Iris.

Having made one blunder, the Professor was not inclined to be precipitate.

"I think I had better consult Hare," he said. "He is an expert linguist and has quite a fair brain, although he may appear irresponsible at times."

"Let's find him at once," urged Iris.

In spite of her haste she stopped to speak impulsively to the vicar's wife.

"Thank you so very much. You don't know what this means to me."

"I'm glad—but why are you thanking me?" asked Mrs. Barnes, in surprise.

Leaving Miss Rose to explain Iris followed the Professor.

Hare was frankly incredulous when they ran him to earth in the restaurant car.

"Bless my soul," he exclaimed, "Miss Froy popping up again? There's something about that good woman that keeps me guessing. I don't mind admitting that I never really believed in the old dear. But what's happened to her?"

The Professor took off his glasses to polish them. Without them his eyes appeared weak, rather than cold, while the painful red ridges on either side of his nose aroused Iris' compassion. She felt quite friendly towards him, now that they were united in a common cause—the restitution of Miss Froy.

"The Misses Flood-Porters didn't want to be drawn in," she declared. "That was clear. But why did those six foreigners all tell lies about her?"

"It must be some misunderstanding," said the Professor nervously. "Perhaps I—"

"No, you didn't," cut in Hare. "You were a clinking interpreter, Professor. You didn't slip up on a thing."

Iris liked him for the ready good nature which prompted him to reassure the Professor, because she was sure that he considered him privately a pompous bore.

"We'll have to play the good old game of 'Spot the lady,'" went on Hare. "My own idea is, she's disguised as the doctor. That black beard is so obvious that she's making it too easy. . . . Or she may be pulling the train, dressed up as a ladylike engine. I'd put nothing past Miss Froy."

Iris did not laugh.

"You're not amusing," she said, "because you seem

to forget that, besides being a real person, she is still missing. We must *do* something."

"Admittedly," agreed the Professor. "But it's a perplexing problem, and I do not care to act without careful consideration."

"He means he wants to smoke," explained Hare. "All right, Professor. I'll take care of Miss Carr, while you squeeze out some brain-juice."

He grinned across the ash-dusted table at Iris, when the Professor had gone.

"Have I got it right?" he asked. "Is this Miss Froy a complete stranger to you?"

"Of course."

"Yet you're nearly going crackers over her. You must be the most unselfish person alive. Really, it's almost unnatural."

"But I'm *not*," admitted Iris truthfully. "It's rather the other way round. That's the amusing part. I can't understand myself a bit."

"Well, how did it start?"

"In the usual way. She was very kind to me—helpful, and all that, so that at first, I missed her because she wasn't at the back of me any more. And then when every one declared I dreamed her, it all turned to a horrible nightmare. It was like trying to explain that every one was out of step but myself."

"Hopeless. But why had you to prove that she was there?"

"Oh, can't you understand? If I didn't, I could never feel that anything, or any one, was *real* again?"

"I shouldn't fly off the handle," remarked Hare stolidly. "I should know it was a post-symptom of brain injury, and therefore perfectly logical."

"But you can't compare your own experience with mine," protested Iris. "You saw a real person and mistook him for the Prince. But I was supposed to have talked to the thin air, while the thin air answered back. . . . I can't tell you what a *relief* it was when Mrs. Barnes remembered her."

She smiled with happiness as she looked out of the window. Now that she was safely anchored to a rational world again, after spinning amid mists of fantasy, the gloomy surroundings had no power to depress her. The afternoon had drawn in early, so that the period of twilight was protracted and it added the final touch of melancholy to the small town through which the express was slowly steaming.

Whenever they crossed a street, Iris could see mean shops, with pitifully shrunken wares—cobbled roads— and glimpses of a soupy swollen river through the gaps between the buildings. The houses—clinging to the rocky hillside, like tufts of lichen on a roof—seemed semi-obliterated by time and weather. Long ago, wood and plaster had been painted grey, but the rain had washed and the sun had peeled some of the walls to a dirty white. Every aspect betrayed poverty and desolation.

"What a horrible place," shuddered Iris, as they passed tall rusty iron gates which enclosed a dock-grown garden. "I wonder who can live here, besides suicides."

"Miss Froy," suggested Hare.

He expected an outburst, but Iris was not listening to him.

"When do we reach Trieste?" she asked.

"Twenty-two-ten."

"And it's five to six now. We mustn't waste any more time. We *must* find her. . . . It sounds exactly like some sloppy picture, but her people are expecting her home. They're old and rather pathetic. And the fool of a dog meets every train."

She stopped—aghast at the sound of her choked voice. To her surprise she found that she was actually affected by the thought of the parents' suspense. As emotion was treason to the tradition of the crowd, she felt ashamed of her weakness.

"I'll have that drink, after all," she declared, blinking the moisture from her eyes. "I feel all mushy—and that's absurd. Old people aren't nearly as pathetic as young ones. They're nearly through—and we've got it all to come."

"You *do* want a drink," agreed Hare. "I'll dig out a waiter."

As he was rising Iris pulled him back.

"Don't go now," she whispered. "There's that horrible doctor."

The spade-bearded gentleman seemed to be searching for some one; and directly his glasses flashed over the young couple his quest was finished. He crossed directly to their table and bowed to Iris.

"Your friend has returned to the carriage," he said.

"Miss Froy?" Iris forgot her repulsion in her excitement. "How marvellous! Where was she?"

He spread his hands and shrugged.

"All the time she was so near. In the next carriage, talking with my nurses."

"Yes," declared Iris, laughing, "that's just where she would be. The first place I ought to have looked in, and didn't."

"Hum." Hare rubbed his chin doubtfully. "It's all very rum. Sure it's the right one?"

"She is the lady who accompanied madame to the restaurant-car," replied the doctor. "A little short lady—not young, but not very old, with a blue feather in her hat."

"That's Miss Froy," cried Iris.

"But why was there all the mystery?" persisted Hare. "No one knowing a thing about her—and all that."

"Ah, that was because we did not understand madame." The doctor shrugged deprecatingly. "She talked so fast and she talked of an English lady. Now the lady is German, maybe, or Austrian—I do not know—but she is not English."

Iris nodded to Hare.

"I made the same mistake, myself, at first," she told him. "She looks anything and she speaks every language. Come on and you shall check up on her."

The journey along the train was growing so familiar that Iris felt she could make it blindfolded. As she passed by the Barnes' compartment she peeped inside. The vicar looked grimly heroic, with folded arms and knotted brow, while his wife showed visible signs of strain. Her eyes were sunken in black circles, but she smiled bravely at Iris.

"Still looking for your friend?" she asked.

"No," called Iris. "She's found."

"Oh, thank God."

"I didn't like that holy woman," Iris confided to Hare as they struggled on again, "but her stock has simply soared with me. She's really kind."

When they reached the reserved coupés, Iris insisted on collecting the Professor, to whom she told her news.

"I want you to come, too, and meet my Miss Froy," she said. "She'll be thrilled when she hears of the sensation she's made."

"A desire to attract attention seems a feminine characteristic," observed the Professor acidly.

Iris only laughed with excitement as her heart gave a sudden bound.

"There she is," she cried. "There she is, at the end of the corridor."

Once again she was overwhelmed by the derided human element as she saw the familiar flat figure in the light tweed suit.

"Miss Froy," she cried huskily.

The lady turned so that Iris saw her face. At the sight she recoiled with a cry of horror.

"That's *not* Miss Froy," she said.

CHAPTER XVI

THE STAR WITNESS

As Iris stared at the face of a stranger, she was plunged back into the inky darkness of the tunnel. She believed that she had emerged into the daylight and her heart was still singing for the joy of deliverance. But she had been deceived by a ray of sunshine striking through a shaft in the roof.

The horror persisted. Blackness was behind her and before—deadening her faculties and confusing her senses. She felt that she was trapped in a nightmare which would go on for ever, unless she could struggle free.

Miss Froy. She must hold on to Miss Froy. At that moment she suddenly remembered her elusive face distinctly in its strange mixture of maturity and arrested youth, with blue saucer eyes and small features all scratched and faded faintly by time.

An impostor stood before her, wearing Miss Froy's oatmeal tweed suit. The face under the familiar hat was sallow—the black eyes expressionless. It looked wooden, as though it could not weep, and had never smiled.

Breaking out of her nightmare, Iris challenged her.

"You are *not* Miss Froy."

"No," replied the woman in English, "I have not heard that name ever before. I am Frau Kummer, as I told you, when we had our tea together."

"That's a lie. I never had tea with you. You're a complete stranger to me."

"A stranger, certainly, such as one meets on a journey. But we talked together. Only a little because your poor head ached."

"*Ah!*"

The significance of the doctor's exclamation was deliberately stressed. It made Iris quiver with apprehension, even while it put her on her guard.

"I mustn't let them get me down," she thought. Then she turned desperately to the Professor.

"This is *not* Miss Froy," she said vehemently.

"The lady has told us that herself," remarked the Professor impatiently. "In fact, with the exception of yourself, no one appears to have heard the somewhat uncommon name of Froy."

It was obvious that he believed that Miss Froy lived at the sign of The Unicorn, in the congenial company of Mrs. Harris and the Spanish prisoner.

"But she's wearing her clothes," persisted Iris, trying to keep her voice from quivering. "Why? *Why?* What's become of Miss Froy? It's some conspiracy—and I'm afraid. . . . She says we had tea together, but we didn't. The waiter knows. Send for him."

To her dismay Hare did not bound off on his mission like a Hermes in nailed boots. Instead, he twisted his lip and looked sheepish.

"Why not call it a day and get some rest?" he suggested in the soothing tone which infuriated Iris.

No one believed her—and the combined force of their incredulity made her doubt herself. The darkness seemed to be closing around her again when she remembered her supporting witness—the vicar's wife.

"Mrs. Barnes," she said faintly.

"I'll fetch her," offered the Professor, who was anxious to put an end to the scene.

Although he was kind-hearted and eminently just—when he knew his bearings—he was prejudiced against Iris, because of an unfortunate incident which marred the close of his last term. One of his most brilliant pupils—a plain, sedate young person, about whose progress he had been almost enthusiastic—had suddenly gone back on him and involved him in a very unpleasant emotional scene.

When she came to his study to wish him good-bye, she had broken down completely, assuring him that she had worked solely to please him, and that she could not face the thought of their parting.

As he had insisted on keeping the door open, from motives of prudence, a version of the affair had been put into circulation, to his intense annoyance. Therefore he cursed his luck in being involved with another hysterical girl, as he passed the coupé occupied by the Misses Flood-Porter.

Through the glass he could see Mrs. Barnes, who had returned to finish her interrupted chat, so he entered.

"More trouble for you, I'm afraid," he warned her. "That very emotional young lady now wants you to identify some one. I wonder if you would mind coming with me to her compartment?"

"Certainly," said Edna Barnes. "Is it the kind little

lady in parchment tweed, speckled with nigger and a blue feather in her hat?"

"Presumably. I seem to recollect the feather." The Professor looked down at her strained brown eyes and added kindly, "You look very pale. Not ill, I hope?"

"Oh, no." Mrs. Barnes' voice was extra cheerful. "It's my husband who is ill. But I'm bearing his pain for him, so that he can sleep."

"Absent treatment?"

"Something of the kind, perhaps. When you're married—if there is a real bond—you share more than an income."

"Well, I call it silly," broke in Miss Rose. "He's far stronger than you are."

The Professor, however, looked at her sweet face with additional respect.

"I don't like to worry you with this matter," he said. "In my opinion, the girl is hysterical and wants to be in the limelight. She says now that the lady is not the original one, who, according to her—is still missing."

"We'll hope she *is* the right one, for your sake," remarked Miss Flood-Porter placidly. "If not, she'll keep you hanging about at Trieste, and you'll miss your connection to Milan."

Mrs. Barnes pressed her hand over her eyes.

"Oh, I hope not," she cried. "My husband wants to get this wretched journey over. Still, one has to do one's duty—whatever the cost."

"But it's so futile," declared Miss Rose. "From your description, this missing governess is no chicken and an experienced traveller. She's either lying low and has given the girl the slip for some good reason of her own, or else it's all moonshine."

"Indubitably the latter," remarked the Professor, as he accompanied Mrs. Barnes out into the corridor.

Here they met the vicar, who had come in search of his wife.

"This *is* my husband," cried Mrs. Barnes, her face lighting up. "Did you think I'd deserted you, Ken?"

While they lingered to chat, Iris sat awaiting the return of Hare with the waiter. She had no real hope of the issue, since she had begun to regard all the officials as being tools of the Baroness. A mysterious power was operating on a wholesale scale, to her own confusion. In proof of this, opposite to her was the horrible changeling who wore Miss Froy's clothing. Yet the incident was inexplicable, since she could find no motive for such a clumsy subterfuge.

Every detail of the woman's figure corresponded so exactly with her recollection of Miss Froy, as she stared at the familiar blue bone buttons, that the first real doubt began to sap her confidence. She asked herself whether she were, in reality, the victim of some hallucination. Hare's story about the Prince proved that it was no uncommon experience.

She was feeling so limp that it seemed almost the easiest way out of her troubles. After all, she would have her work cut out to fight the constant threat of over-hanging illness, without the additional worry of a problematical Miss Froy.

"I shall soon know," she thought, as Hare returned with a waiter in tow.

"You said the chap with the fair hair," he said to Iris.

"I've bagged the only blond in the whole collection. By the way, he is proud of speaking English."

Iris remembered the youth directly she saw the straw-coloured plastered hair and slanting forehead. He wore glasses, and looked more like a student or clerk.

"Do you really understand English?" she asked.

"Certainly, madame," he replied eagerly. "I have my certificates, both for grammar and the conversational test."

"Well, do you remember waiting on me at tea? Have you a reliable memory for faces?"

"Yes, madame."

"Then I want you to look at this lady—" Iris pointed to Kummer and added, "Don't look at her clothes, but look at her face. Now tell me—is that the lady who was having tea with me?"

The waiter hesitated slightly, while his pale eyes grew momentarily blank. Then he nodded with decision.

"Yes, madame."

"You're *sure*?"

"Yes, madame, I am positive sure."

As Iris made no comment, Hare tipped the youth and sent him away. Although the interview had corresponded with his own forecast, he felt acutely uncomfortable. He glanced uneasily at the Baroness and the doctor, but their faces only registered enforced patience, as they waited for the end of the infliction.

Suddenly a muffled cry rang out from the next carriage. Instantly, the doctor sprang up from his seat and hurried back to his patient.

The sound was so unhuman and inarticulate, with its

dulled yet frantic reiteration of "M-m-m-m," that Iris was reminded of some maimed animal, protesting against suffering it could not understand. She had forgotten about the poor broken body—trussed and helpless in the next carriage—lying in complete dependence on two callous women.

The recollection caused all her latent distrust of the doctor to flare up again. She asked herself what awaited the patient at her journey's end? Did she guess that she was being hurried to some operation—doomed to failure, yet recommended solely as an experiment, to satisfy scientific curiosity?

Iris had still sufficient sense to know that she was indulging in neurotic and morbid speculation, so she hurriedly smashed up the sequence of her thoughts. As a characteristic voice told her of the approach of the Professor, she tilted her chin defiantly.

"Mrs. Barnes remembered Miss Froy when all the rest pretended to forget her," she said to Hare. "I know she couldn't tell a lie. So I don't care two hoots for all the rest. I'm banking on *her*."

Edna Barnes advanced, her arm linked within that of her husband, as though for support. As a matter of fact, he was really leaning on her, for the shaking of the train made him feel rather giddy. Although still resolute, his face showed something of the strain of a knight approaching the end of his vigil.

"I understand you want us to identify a friend of yours," he said to Iris, taking command of the situation as a matter of course.

Then he looked down at his wife.

"Edna, my dear," he asked, "is this the lady?"

Unlike the waiter, Mrs. Barnes did not hesitate. Her recognition was instantaneous.

"Yes," she said.

The vicar came forward with outstretched hand.

"I am glad of this opportunity to thank you for your kindness," he said.

Frau Kummer stolidly accepted the tribute paid to Miss Froy. Or—was she really Miss Froy? Iris felt a frantic beating, as though of wings inside her head, as she slipped down into a roaring darkness.

CHAPTER XVII

THERE WAS NO MISS FROY

The immediate effect of Iris' faint was to steady her nerves. When she recovered consciousness, to find some one forcing her head down below the level of her knees, she felt thoroughly ashamed of her weakness. There was not a trace of hysteria in her voice as she apologised.

"Sorry to be such a crashing bore. I'm quite all right now."

"Don't you think you had better lie down?" asked Mr. Barnes. "I'm sure the Miss Flood-Porters would be only too glad to lend you their reserved compartment."

Iris was by no means so sure that the ladies measured up to the vicar's own standard of charity; yet she felt a great need of some quiet place, where she could straighten out the tangle in her brain.

"I want to talk to you," she said to Hare, leaving him to do the rest.

As she anticipated, he jumped at the opportunity.

"Sorry to eject you, Professor," he said, "but our bunny-hutch is booked for the next half-hour."

"Delighted," murmured the Professor grimly.

After swallowing some brandy from the vicar's flask, Iris staggered up from her seat. Her knees felt shaky and her temples were still cold; but the brief period of un-consciousness had relieved the pressure on her heart, so that she was actually better.

As she and Hare—linked together, to the general

inconvenience—lurched down the corridor, she noticed that the lights were now turned on. This arbitrary change from day to night, seemed to mark a distinct stage in the journey. Time was speeding up with the train. The rushing landscape was dark as a blurred charcoal-drawing, while a sprinkle of lights showed that they had reached a civilised zone, of which the wretched little town was the first outpost.

Now that the outside world was shut out, the express seemed hotter and smokier. At first the confined space of the coupé affected Iris with a sense of claustrophobia.

"Open the window wide," she gasped.

"There's plenty of air coming in through the top," grumbled Hare, as he obeyed. "You'll be so smothered in smuts that your own mother wouldn't know you."

"I haven't one," said Iris, suddenly feeling very sorry for herself. "But I'm not here to be pathetic. There's something too real and serious at stake. . . . I want to remind you of something you said this morning at the railway station. You were having an argument with the Professor, and I overheard it. *You* said trial by jury was unfair, because it depended on the evidence of witnesses."

"I did," said Hare. "And I stick to every word."

"And then," went on Iris, "the Professor talked about reliable evidence, and he compared two women. One was English and county—the sort that collects fir-cones and things when she goes for a walk. The other had bought her eyelashes and was dark."

"I remember *her*. Pretty woman, like a juicy black cherry."

"But the Professor damned her. . . . And that's exactly what has happened now. I'm damned as a tainted witness, while he is prejudiced in favour of all those British matrons and Sunday school teachers."

"That's only because they're plain Janes, while you've quite a different face—and thank heaven for it."

Hare's attempt to soothe Iris was a failure, for she flared up.

"I hate my face. It's silly and it means nothing. Besides, why should I be judged on face value if it goes against me? It's not fair. *You* said it wasn't fair. You told the Professor it would lead to a bloody mix-up. . . . You can't blow hot and cold. Unless you're a weather-cock, you've simply got to stand by me."

"All right, I'll stand by. What do you want me to do?"

Iris laid her hot palms on the sticky old-gold plush seat and leaned forward, so that her eyes looked into his.

"I say there *is* a Miss Froy," she told him. "You've got to believe *me*. But my head feels like a three-ring circus, and I've grown confused. Will you go over it with me, so that I can get it clear?"

"I'd like to hear your version," Hare told her.

He smoked thoughtfully as she went over the story of her meeting with the alleged Miss Froy, up to the time of her disappearance.

"Well, you've got one definite fact," he told her. "What the—the lady told you about the big boss is right. I can make an accurate guess as to her employer. At this moment a certain noble Johnny is in the local limelight over charges of bribery, tampering with contracts, and funny little things like that. The latest is he's accused of bumping off the editor of the revolutionary rag which brought the charges."

He picked up a flimsy yellow sheet of badly printed newspaper.

"It's in the stop press," he explained, "but as he was at his hunting-lodge at the time, the final sensation's squashed. However, nobody will bother. It's quite true about the feudal system being in force in these remote districts."

"But it proves me right," cried Iris in great excitement. "How could I know all about her employer, unless Miss Froy told me? And there's something else. When I told Miss Froy about my sunstroke the Baroness was listening. She couldn't know about it in any other way. So Miss Froy *was* there in the carriage with me."

She looked so radiant that Hare hated to crush her confidence.

"I'm afraid," he said, "that it only proves that Frau Kummer was there. *She* told you about her employer, and perhaps a spot of family history when you were having tea with her. Later on, you mentioned your sunstroke to *her*. . . . If you remember, when you came on the train, directly after your sunstroke, you were under the impression that all the other passengers were foreigners. Then you dozed and woke up all confused, and suddenly, Miss Froy, an Englishwoman, comes to life."

"But she had blue eyes and giggled like a schoolgirl," protested Iris. "Besides, there were her old parents and the dog. I couldn't have made *them* up."

"Why not? Don't you ever dream?"

Dejectedly, Iris conceded the point.

"I suppose so. Yes, you must be right."

"I must remind you," continued Hare, "that Kummer was positively identified by the parson as the lady who sent them their tea. Now, I'm the last person to be biased, because all my uncles and fathers are parsons, and I've met them at breakfast—but the Church does imply a definite standard. We insist on parsons having a higher moral code than our own and we try them pretty hard; but you must admit they don't often let us down."

"No," murmured Iris.

"Besides, that parson has such a clinking face. Like God's good man."

"But he never saw Miss Froy," Iris reminded him. "He was speaking for his wife."

Hare burst out laughing.

"You have me there," he said. "Well, that shows how we can slip up. He took the stage so naturally, that he got us all thinking he was the witness."

"If you're wrong over one thing, you can be wrong over another," suggested Iris hopefully.

"True. Let's go into it again. You suggest that the Baroness got rid of Miss Froy—never mind how—and that the other passengers, being local people and in awe of the family, would back her up. So far, you are right. They would."

"Only it seems such a clumsy plot," said Iris. "Dressing up some one quite different and passing her off as Miss Froy."

"But that bit was an eleventh-hour twist," explained Hare. "Remember, you upset their apple-cart, barging in at the last minute. When you made a fuss about Miss

Froy, they denied her existence, at first. You were just a despised foreigner, so they thought they could get away with it. But when you said that other English people had seen her, they had to produce *some one*—and trust to luck that your friends had never heard of Pelman."

He was talking of Miss Froy as though he took her existence for granted. It was such a novelty that, in her relief, Iris' thoughts slipped off in another direction.

"Can't you get that bit of hair to lie down?" she asked.

"No," he replied, "neither by kindness nor threats. It's my secret sorrow. Thank you. That's the first bit of interest you've shown in me."

"Miss Froy is bringing us together, isn't she? You see, you believe in her too."

"Well, I wouldn't go quite so far. But I promised to believe in *you*—false lashes and all—against the Flood-Porter Burberry. In that case, we must accept a plot, inspired by the all-highest, and carried out by his relative, the Baroness—in connection with the doctor, to bump off Miss Froy. . . . So, naturally, that wipes out all the native evidence—train-staff and all."

"You are really rather marvellous," Iris told him.

"Wait before you hand out bouquets. We pass on to the English crowd. The Misses Flood-Porter seem typical John Bulls. What are they like?"

"They've been to the right school and know the best people."

"Are they decent?"

"Yes."

"Then they'd do the decent thing. I'm afraid that is

one up against Miss Froy. . . . Now we'll pass the honey-moon couple—who are presumably not normal—and come to the vicar's wife. What about her?"

"I don't know."

"Remember, you're on oath, and I'm believing *you*."

"Well"—Iris hesitated—"I don't think she could tell a lie."

"And I'm positive she wouldn't. I mix with publicans and sinners and know very little about saints. But, to me, she looks like a real good woman. Besides, she supported you the first time. That shows she has no axe to grind. She said Frau Kummer was the lady who accompanied you to tea. Don't you think we must believe her?"

"I suppose so. . . . Yes."

"Well, then, the weight of evidence is against Miss Froy. But since I've declared my distrust of evidence—however convincing it may sound—I'm going to wash out the lot. To my mind, the whole point is—motive."

Iris saw Miss Froy fading away as Hare went on with his inquisition.

"I understand Miss Froy was quite small beer. Would she be mixed up in any plot?"

"No," replied Iris. "She was against the Red element."

"And neither young nor pretty? So she wasn't kid-napped by the order of the high hat?"

"Don't be absurd."

"Any enemies?"

"No, she boasted of being friends with every one."

"Hum. It's hardly a motive for murder, but was the

family annoyed because she was going to teach in the opposition camp?"

"No. She told me how her employer shook hands with her when he said 'Good-bye,' and thanked her for her services."

"Well—is it clear to you now? Unless you can show me a real motive for a high life conspiracy against a poor but honest governess, I'm afraid there's an end of Miss Froy. Do you agree?"

There was a long pause while Iris tried to battle against the current that was sweeping Miss Froy away. She told herself that so many people, with diverse interests, could not combine to lie. Besides, as Hare had said, what was the motive?

It was useless to struggle any longer and she let herself be swung out with the tide.

"You must be right," she said. "One can't go against *facts*. . . . Yet, she was so real. And her old parents and the dog were real, too."

She had the feeling that she had just slain something fresh and joyous—that fluttered and fought for life—as she added, "You've won. There is no Miss Froy."

CHAPTER XVIII

THE SURPRISE

Mrs. Froy would have been furious had she known that anyone doubted her reality.

While Iris was sighing for the passing of a pleasant ghost, she was at home in the depths of the country, and entertaining friends in her drawing-room.

It was a small room with diamond-paned windows—hung with creepers—which made it rather dark; but in spite of the shabby carpet, it was a gracious place, where odd period chairs fraternised with homely wickerwork, and a beautiful red lacquer cabinet lent the colour which the faded chintz could not supply.

Pots of fine golden chrysanthemums, grown by Mr. Froy, screened the empty iron grate. The guests might have preferred a fire, for there was that slight chill—often associated with old country houses—suggestive of stone flags. Yet the sun could be seen, through the curtain of greenery, shining on the flower-beds outside; for, although the electric lamps were gleaming in the express, the daylight still lingered farther north.

Mrs. Froy was short and stout, with grey hair and great dignity. In addition to having a dominant personality, to-day she felt extra full of vitality. It was born of her excitement at the thought that her daughter was actually on her way home.

The postcard was on the marble mantelshelf, propped up against the massive presentation clock. On its back was printed a crudely coloured picture of mountains, with grass-green bases and white tops, posed against a brilliant blue sky. Scribbled across the heavens, in a round unformed handwriting, was the message:

Home Friday night. Isn't it topping?

Mrs. Froy showed it to her guests.

"Every thing is 'topping' to my daughter," she explained with proud indulgence. "I'm afraid at one time it used to be 'ripping'."

A visitor looked at the string of consonants printed at the base of the picture—shied at them—and compromised.

"Is she *there*?" she asked, pointing to the line.

"Yes." Mrs. Froy reeled off the name rapidly and aggressively. She did it to impress, for it was only the home-interpretation of Winnie's address. But, on her return, their daughter would give them the correct pronunciation, and put them through their paces while they tried to imitate her own ferocious gargling.

Then the room would know more of the laughter on which it had thriven and grown gracious.

"My daughter is a great traveller," went on Mrs. Froy. "Here is her latest photograph. Taken at Budapest."

The portrait was not very revealing since it was expensive. It hinted at the lower half of a small vague face, and a half which photographed very well.

"She looks quite cosmopolitan with her eyes covered by her hat," remarked Mrs. Froy. "Now, this is the Russian one. . . . This one was taken at Madrid, on her birthday. . . . Here she is in Athens."

The collection was chiefly a geographical trophy, for while Mrs. Froy was proud of the printing on the mounts, she secretly resented the middle-aged stranger, who—according to her—was not in the least like her daughter.

She ended the parade by stretching to reach a faded portrait in a silver frame, which stood on a shelf. It was taken at Ilfracombe, and showed a young girl with a slim neck and a smiling face, framed by a mass of curling fair hair. "This is my favourite," she declared. "Now, this really *is* Winnie."

It was the girl who had taught in Sunday school, giggled at churchwardens, and refused her father's curates, before she spread adventurous wings and fluttered away.

But she always returned to the nest.

Mrs. Froy looked again at the clock. She tried to picture Winnie in a grand Continental express, which stamped proudly all over the map of Europe. The poor girl would have to endure two nights in the train, but she always vowed she loved the experience. Besides, she knew all the little dodges of an experienced traveller, to secure comfort.

Although a gregarious soul, Mrs. Froy began to wonder when her guests would go. There had been a hospitable big tea round the dining-room table, with blackberry pie, and a guest had made a stain on the best tablecloth. Although she had guiltily pushed her plate over it, Mrs. Froy had seen it. And since every minute's delay in rubbing salt into the mark would make its removal more difficult, she had found it difficult to maintain the myopia of a hostess.

Besides she wanted to watch the clock alone, and gloat over the fact that every minute was bringing Winnie's return nearer.

Although her fingers were itching to remove the table-cloth, after she had escorted her visitors to the gate, she did not return immediately to the house. In front of her was the field where she gathered mushrooms every morning. It was vividly green, and the black shadows of the elms were growing longer as the sun dipped lower.

It was rather melancholy and lonely, so that she thought of her husband.

"I wish Theodore would come home."

Apparently he heard her wish for he appeared suddenly at the far end of the meadow—his tall thin black figure striding over the grass, as though he were in competition with the elm-shadows.

Around him capered a dog which had some connection with the breed of Old English sheepdog; but his original line had slipped and he was suppressed in the family tree. During a recent hot spell, his shaggy coat had been clipped, transforming him to a Walt Disney creation.

Sock was the herald and toastmaster of the family. Directly he espied the little dumpy grey lady at the garden gate, he made a bee-line towards her and circled around her, barking excitedly to tell her that the master was coming home.

Having done his duty at her end of the field, he tore

back to Mr. Froy with the glad news that the mistress of the house was waiting for him. As he gradually drew them together, both his owners were laughing at his elephantine gambols.

"It must be a great relief to the poor fellow, getting rid of that thatch," said Mr. Froy. "He evidently feels very cool and light now."

"He probably imagines he is a fairy," remarked his wife. "Look at him floating through the air like a puff of thistledown."

"The dear old fool. . . . Won't Winsome laugh?"

"Won't she?"

In imagination, both heard the joyous girlish peal.

"And won't she be thrilled with her room?" went on Mrs. Froy. "Theo, I've a confession. The carpet came when you were out. . . . And I am only human."

Mr. Froy hid his disappointment.

"You mean, you've unpacked it?" he asked. "Well, my dear, I deserved it for running away with Sock, instead of staying and helping you to entertain your visitors."

"Come upstairs and see it. It looks like moss."

They had bought a new carpet for Winifred's bedroom, as a surprise for her return. It represented stringent personal economy, since with a rigid income, any extra purchase meant taking a bite out of the weekly budget.

So he had cut down his allowance of tobacco, and she had given up her rare visits to the cinema. But now that the forty days were over, these good things would have been nothing but ashes and counterfoils.

The carpet remained—a green art-square.

When they reached the bedroom, Mr. Froy looked around him with proud satisfied eyes. It was a typical schoolgirl's bedroom, with primrose washed walls and sepia photogravures of Greuze's beauties—limpid-eyed and framed in dark stained oak. The modern note was there also in photographs of Conrad Veidt and Robert Montgomery, together with school groups and Winnie's hockey-stick.

The faded yellow-rosebud cretonne curtains and bedspread were freshly washed and ironed; a cake of green soap was displayed on the washstand; and two green candles—never to be lit—were stuck into the glass candlesticks before the mirror of the toilet-table.

"We've made it look very nice," said Mr. Froy.

"Yes, but it's not finished yet."

Mrs. Froy pointed to the narrow oak bed, where two lumps at the top and the bottom told of hot-water bottles.

"It won't be finished until there's something inside that bed," she said. "I can't believe that in two nights' time I shall be slipping in to kiss her good-night."

"Only the first night," advised Mr. Froy. "Remember our daughter is the modern girl. Her generation avoids sentiment."

"Yes, for all her heart, Winnie is modern," agreed his wife. "That is why she gets on so well with every one—high and low. You may depend on it, that even on her journey, by now she has made some useful friends who may be helpful at a pinch. I expect she knows all the best people on the train. And by 'best' I mean it in every sense of the word. . . . . I wonder where she is at this moment."

Well for Mrs. Froy that she did not know.

CHAPTER XIX

THE HIDDEN HAND

In the Professor's opinion, the Misses Flood-Porter were representative of the best people. At home he had the reputation of being unsociable and self-sufficient; but directly he travelled he developed a distrust of unfamiliar contacts, and a timidity which sought instinctively the security of his own class.

He wanted to hear his own accent reproduced by some one—however uncongenial—who had been to his college, or lunched at his club, or who knew a cousin of one of his acquaintances.

As he smoked in the corridor after his banishment, he glanced rather wistfully at the compartment where the sisters sat. Miss Rose—although his senior—was sufficiently near his age to be a potential danger. But her face dispelled any fears of dormant hysteria. It was slightly underhung and the firm outline of her protruding lip and chin was reassuring.

Although he recoiled automatically when the elder lady caught his eye and invited him to come in with a smiling gesture, he entered and sat down rather stiffly beside Miss Rose.

"Are you being kept out of your reserved carriage by that girl?" asked Miss Rose bluntly.

When the Professor explained the situation both sisters were indignant.

"Fainted?" Miss Rose's tone was incredulous. "She

was laughing when she passed, arm in arm with that youth. It's all too mysterious for me. Only I sincerely hope she won't stir up a fuss and get us all hung up at Trieste, for nothing."

"It's her dog," explained the elder sister in an aside.

Miss Rose caught her lower lip between her teeth.

"Yes, it's Scottie," she said defiantly. "I'll own up I'm not quite normal over him. But he's so devoted to me—and he pines. The only other person I can trust him to is the butler."

"Strange," remarked the Professor. "My own dog has a marked aversion to butlers. Particularly, to my uncle's."

The social temperature rose several degrees, and Miss Rose grew confidential.

"It's like this. Coles—our butler—is due to go on a cruise, directly I come back. It's a new experience for him and he is thrilled. If I'm overdue he will probably stay at home with Scottie, and, of course, I don't want him to lose his holiday. . . . On the other hand, if he went, poor little Scottie would be frantic. He would feel he had lost every friend."

"We have an excellent staff," supplemented Miss Flood-Porter, "but, unfortunately, none of them likes animals."

The Professor's long face wrinkled up in a smile which made him resemble a benevolent horse.

"I can enter into your feelings," he told them. "I confess that my own dog makes me lose my sense of proportion. I rarely go abroad, because I cannot take her with me owing to quarantine regulations. But this year a complete change seemed indicated."

The sisters exchanged glances.

"Isn't that strange?" declared Miss Flood-Porter. "That is exactly our own position."

Miss Rose flinched and changed the subject quickly.

"What's your dog?" she asked.

"Sealyham. White."

The Professor was sitting bolt upright no longer. Introduced by butlers, and their friendship cemented by the common ownership of dogs, he felt he was in congenial company. So he relaxed to gossip.

"A position of responsibility towards that extraordinary young lady seems to have been thrust upon me," he said. "She appears bent on making things very awkward for every one. I understand she was staying at the same hotel as you. . . . What opinion did you form of her?"

"Don't ask me," said Miss Rose bluntly. "I'm prejudiced. So, perhaps, I shouldn't be fair."

Her sister made the explanation.

"We know nothing about *her*, but she was with a party of near-nudists, who drank all day and night, and were a complete nuisance. The noise was worse than a pneumatic road-drill. And we came so far especially to get perfect rest and quiet."

The Professor clicked.

"I quite understand your feelings," he said. "The point is—did she strike you as hysterical?"

"I only know there was a disgraceful scene on the lake yesterday. Two women screaming about a man. She was one."

"I'm not surprised," commented the Professor. "At present she is either telling a pack of lies to get into the limelight, or she is suffering from slight delirium as a result of sunstroke. The latter is the charitable view. But it involves responsibility. After all, we are her compatriots."

Miss Rose began to fidget. When she opened her case and drew out a cigarette, her fingers were not quite steady.

"Suppose—she is telling the truth?" she asked. "It's not fair for us to leave the girl behind us at Trieste without any backing. . . . I'm worried stiff not knowing what to do."

Had Mrs. Froy been listening, she would have clapped her gouty old hands. At last Miss Rose's attitude was coming into line with her expectations. The best people would be looking after Winnie. So no harm could possibly come to her. . . . But all the same, "Keep her safe—and bring her home to us."

Unfortunately the Professor was proof against the power of prayer. He wrinkled up his face in a sceptical grimace.

"Her story is too unfounded for me to credit it," he said. "But even if the vanished governess were not a myth, I cannot conceive any cause for anxiety on her behalf. Her disappearance must be voluntary, because if she had come to any harm, or met with an accident, it would have been notified at once by an eye-witness."

"Exactly," agreed Miss Flood-Porter. "The train is so crowded that if she knew the ropes, she could play 'hide and seek' indefinitely with the ticket-collector."

"Therefore," summed up the Professor, "if she *is* hiding, she must have some strong personal reason for such a course. My own feeling is never to interfere with private issues. It would be extremely tactless and inconsiderate of us to start a general search for her."

Miss Rose drew deeply at her cigarette.

"Then you don't think me definitely feeble to put Scottie's interests first?" she asked.

"I should consider that you were letting your dog down if you sacrificed him to such an absolutely preposterous issue," replied the Professor.

"That goes for me. Thank you, Professor." Miss Rose examined her firm pink hands. "I'm smutty. I'd better wash."

When she had lurched out into the corridor, Miss Flood-Porter spoke to the Professor confidentially.

"I couldn't mention it before my sister—she is so sensitive on the subject—but we've just been through a nerve-shattering experience. It was the result of interfering in other people's business. And I don't see that we did a pennorth of good. . . . Am I boring you?"

"Not in the least."

Miss Flood-Porter began her story of those events which played their part in shaping the conduct of the sisters, and so—indirectly—affected the destiny of a stranger.

"We live in a very quiet neighbourhood, close to the cathedral. It was ruined for every one when a terrible person came to live there. A War profiteer—at least, I call them all that. One day, when he was scorching in his car—drunk, as usual—he knocked down a woman.

148

We saw the accident, and our evidence got him six months' imprisonment, as it was a bad case."

"I congratulate you on your public spirit."

"I'm afraid we, too, were quite pleased with ourselves, until he came out. After that we were marked people. This man—aided by his two boys—persecuted us in every kind of way. Windows were smashed—flower beds raided—horrible things thrown over the garden walls—obscene messages chalked on the gates. We could never catch them in the act, although we appealed to the police and they had a special watch kept on the premises. . . . After a time it got on our nerves. It did not matter where we were, or what we were doing, we were always listening for another crash. It affected my sister most, as she was terrified lest one of her pet animals might be the next victim. Luckily, before it came to that, the man left the town."

Miss Flood-Porter stopped, overcome by the memories she had raised.

It began on the morning when she went out into the garden, to find that her unique white delphiniums had been uprooted during the night.

After that there was the ever-increasing tension—the constant annoyance—the cumulative pecuniary loss—the futility of repairs, when panes of glass were replaced, only to be smashed again. It was like standing at a crossroads in windy weather and being buffeted by an invisible weathercock, which whirled round again after it had struck its blow. There were flutters of apprehension whenever the fiendish boys scorched by them on their bicycles, grinning with impudent triumph. And the time came when their nerve was worn down, so that their imaginations raced away with them and they grew fearful of worse evils in store.

It ended on the evening when Miss Flood-Porter found her sister Rose in tears. If the Rock of Gibraltar had suddenly shaken like a jelly, she could not have been more aghast.

She looked up to meet the Professor's sympathetic eye.

"Can you blame us," she asked, "when I tell you that, after that, we made a vow never to interfere in anything again—unless it was a case of cruelty to animals or children?"

As Iris passed the window, in token that he was free to return to his own compartment, the Professor rose.

"Tell your sister," he advised, "not to worry any more, but to get back to her dog as quickly as possible. No one is going to suffer in any way. In case of any further complications, you can trust me to take charge."

A few minutes later, when Miss Flood-Porter repeated the message, Miss Rose was greatly relieved.

"Now I can go home to Scottie with a *clear* conscience," she said. "Anyone must have complete confidence in the Professor."

She forgot one important point. The Professor was working on the basis that Miss Froy was a fiction of hysteria—while both the sisters had seen her in the flesh.

CHAPTER XX

STRANGERS INTERVENE

After Miss Froy had shrivelled to a never-never, Iris was thrown back on herself again. When her first relief at shelving the riddle had passed, she grew worried by her own sensations. Her knees were shaky, while her head felt light and empty as a blown eggshell.

Miss Froy would have known that, in addition to the after-effects of sunstroke, the girl was exhausted for lack of light nourishment. At this juncture she was a dead loss to Iris, for Hare—with the best intentions—could only offer stimulants.

As she clung to the shaking rail, fighting off recurrent spells of giddiness, Iris told herself that she must forcibly hang out until she reached Basle.

"It would be fatal if I collapsed," she thought fearfully. "Max is too young to be any good. Some busybody would push me out at the first station, and pack me off to the local hospital."

And anything might happen to her there, as in Miss Froy's terrible story. Or did Frau Kummer tell it to her?

It was an ordeal to stand, but although she had insisted on leaving Hare—when she found that both talking and listening had become a strain—she shrank from the thought of return to her own compartment. It was too near the doctor and too remote from her compatriots. At the far end of the corridor she felt bottled up in enemy territory.

Besides—it was haunted by the ghost of a little tweed spinster, of whom it was not wise to think too long.

The high-pitched conversation of the Misses Flood-Porter—audible through the open door—was a distraction.

"I've written to Captain Parker, to meet us with his car at Victoria, to push us through the Customs," said Miss Flood-Porter.

"Hope he'll be there," fussed Miss Rose. "If he fails us, we may lose our connection. And I've written to Cook that dinner is to be ready at seven-thirty to the dot."

"What did you order?"

"*Not* chicken. Definitely. It will be some time before I can endure one again. I said a nice cutlet of salmon and a small leg of lamb. Peas, if possible. If it is too late for them, French beans and marrow. I left the sweet to Cook."

"That sounds very good. I'm longing to eat a plain English dinner again."

"So am I."

There was a short pause before Miss Rose began to worry anew.

"I do hope there'll be no muddle over our wagon-lits at Trieste."

"Oh, my dear," cried her sister, "don't suggest such a thing. I couldn't face the idea of sitting bolt upright all night. Didn't you hear the manager telephone for them?"

"I stood by him while he was doing it. Of course, I could not understand anything. But he assured me positively that they were being reserved for us."

"Well, we must hope for the best. . . . I've been looking through my engagement-book. It's the Bishop's last garden party, the day after we get back."

"Oh, we *couldn't* miss that."

Iris' half-smile was bitter as she listened to the characteristic chatter of two inexperienced women-travellers, who felt very far from their beaten track.

"And I expected *them* to risk losing their reservations and spoiling their dinner," she thought. "What a hope!"

Once again she flattened herself against the window, as the flaxen-haired waiter came down the corridor. Miss Rose saw him pass for she bounded out after him.

"Stop," she cried in her most imperious tone. "You speak English?"

"Yes, madame."

"Then get me some matches, please. Matches."

"Oh, yes, madame."

"I wonder if he really understood her," thought Iris, who had grown sceptical of every one.

Her doubts were unfounded, for after a brief interval the waiter returned with a box of matches. He used one to light Miss Rose's cigarette and handed her the remainder, with a bow.

"The engine-driver is fulfilling his obligations and the express will reach Trieste within the scheduled time," he informed Miss Rose, who remarked, "Oh, definitely good."

He seemed anxious to oblige every one. When Iris in her turn called out to him, he wheeled round smartly as though eager for service.

As he recognised her, however, a change came over his face. His smile faded, his eyes shifted, and he appeared to conquer an impulse to bolt.

All the same he listened obediently as she gave her order.

"I'm not going to the dining-car for dinner," she told him. "I want you to bring me something to my carriage—right at the end of the corridor. A cup of soup or Bovril, or Ovaltine. Nothing solid. You understand?"

"Oh, yes, madame."

He bowed himself away. But he never brought the soup. . . .

Iris forgot her order directly she had given it. A stream of passengers had begun to file steadily past her, crushing her against the side of the corridor. Since every one was heading in the same direction, she glanced at her watch.

The time told her that the first dinner was about to be served.

"Only three hours now to Trieste," she thought gladly—goaded no longer by the thought of wasted minutes.

Where she stood she was very much in the way of the procession, and—since the majority was hungry—she was resented as an obstacle. She met with ruthless treatment, but it was useless to fight her way out against the human current. When she made the attempt she was nearly knocked down, as some of the rougher element began to push.

No one appeared to notice her plight as she tried to get out of the jam. The train was racing at top speed, and she was shaken and bruised as she gripped the rail. Terrified of being crushed, her palms were sticky and her heart leaped with panic.

At last the pressure was relaxed and she breathed more freely, as she waited for the better-behaved passengers to pass. Presently a combination of strokes, dots and dashes, in black and white, told her that the family party—linked together—was on its way to dinner. Free from the restraining presence of the Baroness, they talked and laughed, evidently in high spirits at the prospect of their meal.

Although the parents were sufficiently big to inflict some merciless massage as they squeezed past her, Iris was glad to see them, for she argued that they must be in the tail of the procession. Then the blonde slipped by—cool as a dripping icicle—with unshatterable composure and without one ruffled hair.

Although the corridor was practically clear, Iris still lingered, unable to face the prospect of being alone in the carriage with the Baroness. To her relief, however, the personage herself came in sight, accompanied by the doctor. Sure of getting a seat in the dining-car—however late her entrance—she had waited for the mob to disperse.

As her vast black figure surged past Iris, a simile floated into the girl's mind. An insect and a relentless foot.

The doctor threw her a keen professional glance which noted each symptom of distress. With a formal bow he passed on his way, and she was able to bump and sway along the corridors, back to the empty carriage.

She had barely seated herself, after an involuntary

glance at Miss Froy's empty corner, when Hare hurried in.

"Coming to first dinner?" he asked. "I warn you, the second one will be only the scrapings."

"No," she told him, "the waiter's bringing me some soup here. I've been in a rough-house and I simply couldn't stand the heat."

He looked at her as she wiped her damp brow.

"Gosh, you look all in. Let me get you a spot. No? . . . Well, then, I've just had an intriguing experience. On my way here, a woman's trembling hand was laid on my sleeve and a woman's piteous voice whispered, 'Could you do something for me?' I turned and looked into the beautiful eyes of the vicar's wife. Needless to say, I pledged myself to the service of the distressed lady."

"Did she want a hot-water bottle for her husband?" asked Iris.

"No, she wanted me to send a telegram for her directly we reached Trieste. But now comes the interesting bit. I'm not to let her husband know or suspect anything. After that, I can't hint at the message."

"Who wants to know it?" asked Iris dully.

"Sorry. I see you really are flat. I won't worry you any more. Chin-chin."

Hare left the compartment, only to pop his head again round the corner of the door.

"There's the ugliest ministering angel I've ever seen in the next carriage," he told her. "But what I really came back for was this. Do you know who Gabriel is?"

"An archangel."

"I see. You're definitely *not* in the know."

As the time passed and no waiter appeared with her soup, Iris came to the conclusion that he was too rushed to remember her order. But she felt too limp to care. All that mattered was the crawling hands of her watch, which drew her imperceptibly nearer to Trieste.

As a matter of fact, the fair waiter possessed a heart of gold, together with a palm which twitched as instinctively as a divining-twig in the direction of a tip. He would have found time to rush in that cup of soup, whatever the demand on his resource. The only drawback was that he knew nothing about the order.

Like most of his fellow-countrymen, he had been made a good linguist by the method of interchange between families of different nationalities. As he was ambitious, he felt that one extra language might turn the scale in his favour, when he applied for a job. Accordingly, he learned English from his teacher, who had taught himself the language from a book of phonetic pronunciation.

The waiter, who was an apt pupil, passed his school examination and was able to rattle off strings of English phrases; but the first time he heard the language spoken by a Briton he was unable to understand it.

Fortunately English tourists were rare and most of their conversation was limited to the needs of their meals. While his ear was growing accustomed, therefore, he managed to keep his job by bluff and by being a good guesser.

Miss Rose's unlighted cigarette gave him the clue that she wanted matches. Moreover her voice was loud and she was brief.

But in Iris he met his Waterloo. Her low husky voice and unfamiliar words beat him completely. After his first nerve-racking experience, he could only fall back on the mechanical "Yes, madame," and rush to take cover.

Before the other passengers returned to the carriage, Iris had another visitor—the Professor. He took off his glasses to polish them nervously, while he explained the nature of his mission.

"Hare has been talking to me, and—frankly—he is worried about you. I don't want to alarm you. Of course, you are not ill—that is, not definitely ill—but we are wondering if you are fit to continue the journey alone."

"Of course I am," cried Iris in a panic. "I'm perfectly fit. And I don't want anyone to worry on my account."

"Yet, if you should collapse later, it would be decidedly awkward for you and every one. I was discussing it with the doctor, just now, and he came to the rescue with an admirable suggestion."

As he paused, Iris' heart began to flutter with apprehension, for she knew by instinct what the proposal would be.

"The doctor," went on the professor, "is taking a patient to a hospital at Trieste, and he offers to see you safely placed in a recommended nursing-home for the night."

CHAPTER XXI

LIES

As the Professor made his proposal, Iris saw the opening of the trap. But he had forgotten the bait. She was a free agent—and nothing could induce her to walk inside.

"I will not go anywhere with that doctor," she said.

"But—"

"I refuse to discuss it."

The Professor seemed about to argue, so she decided that it was no time for politeness.

"I can't pretend to be grateful for your interest," she told him. "I consider it interference."

The Professor stiffened at the last word.

"I have not the slightest wish to be intrusive," he said. "But Hare was genuinely concerned about you, and he asked me to use my influence."

"No one can influence me to go with that horrible doctor."

"In that case there is no more to be said."

The Professor was only too thankful to be rid of his responsibility. Since the girl was bent on antagonising those who held out a helping hand, there would be time for a smoke, while he waited for the second dinner.

Iris did not like the Professor's face, but his Harris-tweed back was British and reassuring. She realised with a pang that she was sending it away.

Acting on impulse she called him back.

"I won't go with that doctor," she said. "He's like

death. But—supposing I *should* flop—which is absurd—I'd go with *you*."

She thought she was making a concession, but at that there were two frightened people in the carriage.

"That is impossible," said the Professor sharply, to hide his nervousness. "The circumstances put it out of court. The doctor has made you a kind and helpful offer —which comes best from a medical man."

He opened the door of the trap again, but she shook her head. She would never go inside. Unless—of course —she were tricked.

It was a disquieting reflection, for she was beginning to think that she could trust no one. Even Hare had let her down. While he was, in reality, concerned about her condition, he had been facetious about Mrs. Barnes. According to him, she had asked him to send a telegram to some man called "Gabriel," while her husband was to be kept in the dark.

Since it was impossible to connect the vicar's wife with a clandestine affair, Iris concluded that Hare had been trying to pull the wool over her eyes.

She resented the feebleness of the effort, especially as Mrs. Barnes was connected with a poignant memory. It was she who had driven away Miss Froy and sent her groping back into Limbo.

Iris could not forgive her for that, for she was missing badly the support which only the little governess could give. At this juncture, she knew she would be safe in those experienced hands. She felt terrified, sick, friend-less—for she had burned her bridges.

Besides, whenever she thought about the mystery, she

felt near the border-line of that world which was filled with shifting shadows—where phantasy usurped reality, and she existed merely in the Red King's dream. Unless she kept a firm grip on herself, her sanity might hang—or crash—on the fact of Miss Froy's existence.

There were others in that trainful of holiday folk who were in a worse plight than herself. One was the invalid in the next carriage. Although she was chiefly unconscious, the flash of every lucid second held the horror of the shock which had stunned her into darkness. And if the moment lasted a fraction too long, there was time for a cloud of awful doubts to arise.

"Where am I? What is going to happen to me? Where are they taking me?"

Luckily, before these questions could be answered, the flare always died down again. So, therefore, she was in better case than Edna Barnes, who was in full possession of her faculties while she endured a protracted martyrdom of mental suffering.

She had been completely happy in anticipation of their last mountain ramble when she saw the letter in the pigeon-hole of the bureau. Her mother-in-law's handwriting gave her a warning pang which broke slightly the shock of the contents of the note.

"I've been wondering what to do for the best," wrote the excellent lady. "I don't want to make you anxious during your long journey, yet, on the other hand, I feel I ought to prepare you for a disappointment. I had hoped to have Gabriel in perfect health for your return, and up to now he's been splendid. But now he has developed a cold in his chest. He is quite comfortable and the doctor says he is going on as well as can be expected. So there is no need for you to worry."

Edna Barnes skimmed the letter in a flash which read between the lines. If her mother-in-law had composed it with a view to alarm her, she could not have succeeded better. All the familiar soothing phrases were there. "No need to worry." "As well as can be expected." "Comfortable"—the hospitable formula for a hopeless case.

A cold on the chest could camouflage bronchitis or even pneumonia; and she had heard that a big strong baby, stricken by these complaints, was sometimes snuffed out after a few hours' illness. Her heart nearly burst as she wondered whether, at that moment, he were already dead.

Then her husband called out to inquire the contents of the letter. The answer had been "Margaret Rose silk."

She had lied with a fierce protective instinct to save him from her own agony. There was no need for two to suffer, if she could bear his pain for him. Screening her torment with her habitual smile, she racked her brains desperately for some reason to leave for England that same day.

Just as the vicar took the packet of sandwiches from her, preparatory to their start, she snatched at the excuse of Miss Rose Flood-Porter's warning dream.

Although he was disappointed, the vicar gave way to her in the matter. The sisters, too, decided to take no chances, when they heard that the vicar's wife had changed her plans owing to superstitious presentiments. As the honeymoon couple had previously decided to go, the exodus from the hotel was complete.

For the first time Edna Barnes was glad that her husband suffered from train-sickness. While he sat with closed eyes and gritted teeth, she had some respite from acting. Her only consolation was knowing that she was on her way home. Therefore, when she was threatened with the prospect of an enforced delay at Trieste, she felt desperate.

She was faced with the first real test of her principles—and her conscience won. Deception to save her husband from unnecessary suffering was a form of the lie magnificent. But now she told herself that the cause of humanity must come before family ties, because it was selfless.

She was prepared to do her duty—whatever the cost—by Miss Froy. But when she was assured by those whose judgment she could trust, that the peril was negligible, her resolution slipped.

The cause was too inadequate to exact such a sacrifice. On the evidence, it was nothing but the trumped-up invention of a hysterical girl to attract notice. But Gabriel was ill. He needed her, and he won.

It was after she had identified Frau Kummer as Miss Froy that she suddenly realised the advantage of a willing young man who could send off a telegram to her mother-in-law. As she doubted whether she could receive the reply without her husband's knowledge—since her name might be bawled out by some official—she asked for the latest bulletin to await her at Calais. The sea-crossing would revive the vicar, while it would not be kind to keep him in the dark until he reached home.

Although her eyes were tragic, she smiled faintly at the thought of his unconsciousness. Like a big baby he was sorry for his aches and pains, but he knew nothing of what he was spared.

"Only a mother knows," she thought.

This was exactly Mrs. Froy's own conviction as she sat in the twilight and hungered for her child's return.

CHAPTER XXII

KILLING TIME

As a rule, Mrs. Froy lived on the sunny side of the street. This evening, however, the long black shadows of the elms seemed to have stretched out to reach her mind, for she was unaccountably depressed.

The sun no longer shone greenly through the creepers which muffled the windows, but she was accustomed to gloom. For reasons of economy, the lamp was never lit until the last possible moment. Neither was she influenced by the melancholy of the view from her bedroom, which overlooked a corner of the churchyard.

Having dwelt in rectories for so long, it was second-habit for the Froys to live close to the church. Whenever she looked out at the slanting tombstones of forgotten dead, she had trained herself to picture a spectacular resurrection, when the graves suddenly burst open and their glorified contents shot up into the air like a glittering shower of rockets.

This evening, when the green had all turned grey, she had her first misgivings.

"I wonder if it's healthy for us to sleep so near all those mouldering corpses."

In ordinary circumstances she would have scoffed at her idea; but she could not dislodge the black monkey that sat on her shoulder. Vague misgivings and presentiments kept shaking through her mind.

She told herself that she would be profoundly grateful

when Winnie was safely home. Travel must be risky—otherwise railway companies would not issue insurance policies. Suppose Winnie were taken ill on the journey and had to be dumped in some foreign waiting-room.

Anything might happen to her—a smash, or even worse. One read of terrible things which happened to girls travelling alone. Not that Winnie was actually a girl—thank goodness—but she was so young for her age.

At this point Mrs. Froy took herself in charge.

"Only two nights more," she reminded herself. "You ought to be happy as a queen, instead of carrying on like a weeping-willow with a stomach ache. Now, you find out what's at the bottom of all this."

Before long she believed she had worked back to the original cause of her depression. It was the blackberry stain on the best tablecloth, which had not yielded entirely to salt.

"Goose," she said. "It'll boil out in the wash."

Making a face at the tombstones, she stumped out of the room and down the stairs in search of her husband.

Contrary to custom she found him in the parlour sitting in the dark.

"Lazybones, why haven't you lit the lamp?" she asked.

"In a minute." Mr. Froy's voice was unusually lifeless. "I've been brooding. Bad habit. . . . It's an extraordinary thing that Winsome has been away so often, yet this is the first time I've ever felt apprehensive about her safety. These Continental trains—I suppose I'm growing old. The ground is pulling me."

Mrs. Froy's heart gave a sudden leap as she listened. So he, too, had caught the warning whisper.

Without speaking, she struck a match, turned up the wick of the lamp, lit it, and fitted on the chimney. As she waited for the glass to warm through, she looked at her husband's face, visible in the weak glow.

It appeared white, bloodless and bony—the face of a man who should be going to bed in a damp corner under the window, instead of sharing her spring-mattress.

At the sight she exploded with the righteous wrath of a woman who is rough on shadows.

"Never let me hear you talk like that again," she scolded. "You're as bad as Miss Parsons. She's only sixty-six, yet the last time we came back from town together, she grumbled because the bus was full and she had to stand. I said, 'My dear, don't let every one know that you are not accustomed to Court circles.' And then I said, 'Take my seat. *I'm* young.'"

"Did the people in the bus laugh?" asked Mr. Froy appreciatively.

In the circle of mellow lamplight his face had lost its pallor. Before she replied, his wife pounced on the window-cords and rattled the green window-curtains together, shutting out the bogie-twilight.

"Yes," she said, "they simply roared. Then some one started to clap. But when I thought the joke had gone far enough, I stopped it. . . . I *looked* at them."

Although Mrs. Froy was proud of her gifts as a comedian, her sense of dignity was stronger. Her head was held high, as though she were still quelling her audience, as she inquired, "Where is Sock?"

"My dear, I'm afraid he is waiting outside until it is time to meet the train. I do wish I could make the poor fellow understand it's Friday."

"I'll make him," announced Mrs. Froy. "Sock."

The big dog shambled in immediately, for although normally too spoiled to be obedient, he always respected a certain rasp in his mistress' voice.

Mrs. Froy took three biscuits from the tin and laid them in a row on the fender-stool.

"Look, darling," she said. "Mother's got three biscuits for you. This is to-night, but Winnie's not coming to-night. This is to-morrow, but Winnie's not coming to-morrow. *This* is Friday, and Winnie's coming Friday and you shall go and meet the train. . . . Remember— *this* one."

Sock looked up at her as though he were straining to understand—his amber eyes beaming with intelligence under his wisps of hair, for his head had not been shorn.

"He understands," declared Mrs. Froy. "I can always talk to animals. Perhaps our vibrations are the same. I know what's in his mind and I can always make him know what is in mine."

She turned back to the fender-stool and picked up the first biscuit.

"This is to-night," she explained. "Well, to-night's over. So you can eat to-night."

Sock entered into the spirit of the game. While he was making a mess of crumbs on the mat, Mrs. Froy spoke to her husband.

"That's an end of to-night for us, too," she said. "And good riddance. I wish you would remember that it's bad form to go half-way to meet troubles which are not coming to your house, and which have no intention of calling on you. . . . What are you grinning at?"

Shaking with laughter, Mr. Froy pointed to Sock, who was in the act of crunching the last biscuit.

"'*He* understands,'" he quoted with gentle mockery.

The sight of his face made Mrs. Froy forget her momentary discomfiture. It looked years younger. There was no question now of where he ought to sleep that night.

She patted Sock, kissed his nose and flicked the biscuit crumbs from his coat. "Yes," she said tartly, "he understands—and better than you do. Don't you see that he is trying to make the time pass quicker?"

CHAPTER XXIII

STAKE YOUR COUNTER

At that moment others besides Mrs. Froy were anxious to speed up the march of time. Some were on the express which was being stoked up for its final spurt, to reach Trieste on time.

One of these—Mrs. Todhunter—hid her impatience under a pose of nonchalance. Wherever she went, she attracted notice and she also excited feminine envy by her special atmosphere of romance. Apparently she had everything that a woman could want—beauty, poise, exquisite clothes, and a wealthy, distinguished bridegroom.

In reality she was feverishly eager to get back to her husband.

He was a stout middle-aged building-contractor, named Cecil Parmiter. When at home Mrs. Laura Parmiter lived in a super-fine new house, with all those modern improvements which her husband introduced into the blocks of flats he built for others—and with none of their shortcomings. She had a comfortable income, a generous allowance, competent servants, leisure, a trusting affectionate husband and two large children.

She had the additional detail of respectability.

Although she was the social queen of her set, she was secretly ambitious and discontented. During the rehearsals of a local pageant, when class-distinctions were levelled, she met a certain rising barrister—a visitor to the district, who had been roped into taking a part. He was a king and she was a queen—and the royal atmosphere lent a glamour to their meetings.

He was infatuated—temporarily—by her statuesque beauty and the facility with which she could quote passages from Swinburne and Browning, culled from her Oxford Book of Verse. After a few meetings in London, under the seal of the apple, he swept her away with him on a passionate adventure.

Although she lost her footing, Mrs. Laura's brain still functioned. She had a definite ulterior motive for her surrender. During a session of Browning lectures, she had read "The Statue and the Bust" and had imbibed its spirit. She determined, therefore, to risk her counter on a bold fling—the chance of a double divorce.

After the preliminary patch of mud was crossed, she would take her rightful place in Society as the beautiful wife of a distinguished barrister. The world soon forgets—while she was confident that she could compel her husband to admit her moral claim to the children.

She lost. . . . And Browning could have been proud of the spirit in which she took her toss.

The barrister was married to a sour elderly wife; but she possessed both a title and wealth. When Mrs. Laura discovered that he had not the slightest intention of making their adventure a prelude to matrimony, her pride forbade her to show any disappointment.

Perhaps her nonchalance was easier to assume by reason of her own disillusionment. The passionate adventure had not matured according to its promise. It taught her that a professional man did not differ so greatly from a tradesman in essentials and that they looked much the same before shaving and without their collars.

Moreover, the barrister had a handicap from which the builder was immune. He was a hard snorer.

To make matters worse, while he was careless of his own failings, his standard for women was so fastidious that she found it a strain to live up to it. She could never relax, or be natural, without being conscious of his criticism or impatience.

Being practical, she determined to cut short the holiday and get back to her husband while the going was good. Fortunately, she had not burned any bridges. Her husband had bought her return ticket to Turin, and she had told him to expect no mail, since he was going on a sea trip to the Shetlands.

Her plan was to leave the barrister at Turin, where he had joined her on the outward journey, and to stay there, for a night, so that her luggage could display the hotel labels.

The end of it all would be a happy domestic reunion and a better understanding, for—by contrast—she had learnt to appreciate her husband's solidity. Thus one more matrimonial shipwreck had been averted by a trial-venture and a smashed code of morality.

As the Todhunters sat in their coupé, waiting for the second dinner to be served, they were a spectacle which attracted the interest of the tourists who straggled past the window. They must still be known by the name in which they had registered, since the barrister was too cautious to sign his own name.

It was "Brown."

However, his parents had done their best for him, and his title of "Sir Peveril Brown" was sufficiently well-known to be dangerous—in addition to a striking profile which had been reproduced often in the pictorial Press.

True to her character of Browning good loser, Mrs. Laura continued to play her part. Although her acquired drawl was replaced sometimes by her natural accent she still looked choice and aloof as a beautiful princess—remote from the rabble. But her fingers kept tapping the greasy old-gold plush seat, while she glanced continuously at her watch.

"Still hours and hours," she said impatiently. "It seems as though we'd never make Trieste—let alone Turin."

"Anxious to drop me?" asked Todhunter incredulously.

"I'm not thinking of you. . . . But children get measles—and deserted husbands prove unfaithful. The world is full of pretty typists."

"In that case, he'd have nothing on you, if it came to a show-up."

She started at the word.

"*Show-up?* Don't give me the jitters," she cried sharply. "There's no chance of it, is there?"

He stroked his lip.

"I should say we are reasonably secure," he told her. "Still. . . I've handled some queer cases in my career. One never knows what will break. It was unfortunate that there were any English visitors at the hotel. And you are entirely too beautiful to remain anonymous."

Mrs. Laura shook off his hand. She wanted reassurance, not compliments.

"You told me there was no risk," she said. Forgetting that her original scheme had been to force her husband to take action, she added bitterly, "What a fool I've been!"

"Why are you suddenly so anxious to get back to your husband?" asked Todhunter.

"Well, to be brutally frank, we are all of us out for what we can get. And he can give me more than you can."

"Haven't I given you a memory you'll never forget?"

Mrs. Laura's eyes flashed angrily, and Todhunter laughed. He had grown rather bored by the languid beauty and her synthetic culture; but now that she had suddenly become alive, he was aware of the fact that she was slipping away from him.

"I was only teasing you," he said. "Of course, no one will ever know about us. *I* could risk nothing like that. . . . But we might have been in a jam if I had not thought a jump ahead when that girl asked me about the peeping woman."

"Why?" asked Laura, who had only grasped the fact that Todhunter would never go an inch out of his way to champion an unattractive middle-aged woman.

"Why? Because she's disappeared. If I had not repudiated her, I should have to make a statement at Trieste," Todhunter laughed. "Can't you see the headlines? 'Englishwoman lost on Continental express.'

Photograph of Mr. Todhunter who was on his honey-moon, when. . . And thus and thus. It wouldn't be long before the English Press got on to my identity. One of the penalties of fame—however limited."

Mrs. Laura did not look as impressed as he wished, for his words had raised a new issue.

Perhaps, after all, the game was not lost, because it was not yet ended. Although Todhunter had no inten-tion of risking a scandal when he lured her away on this trip, she saw a chance to engineer one and so force his hand.

If she went to the Professor and assured him of Miss Froy's existence the result was bound to be future com-plications. There could be no doubt of the Professor's probity and public spirit, which would enforce an inves-tigation—whatever the cost to his personal convenience.

Her violet eyes suddenly glittered. As the beautiful bride of the alleged Todhunter, she was an important detail in the picture, and one that reporters would not overlook or suppress. She always made such an appeal-ing photograph.

Afterwards there would be a sensational divorce case, and Sir Peveril—in honour bound—would be obliged to make her the second Lady Brown.

At the thought she drew a deep breath, for the wheel was still spinning.

Her counter was not yet lost.

CHAPTER XXIV

THE WHEEL SPINS

Mrs. Laura sat and looked at the window which held the reflection of the lighted carriage, thrown on panels of rushing darkness. She smiled at her dimly-mirrored face—smoky-dark, with shadowed eyes and triumphant lips. The wheel was still spinning for her.

And since their fates were interlinked it was spinning also for Miss Froy. The little spinster was in a perilous plight, but she was an obstinate optimist. She clung to the hope that everything would come right in the end, and that at long last she would reach home.

Miss Froy loved her home with that intense perverted passion which causes ardent patriots to desert their native lands and makes men faithless to their wives. Like them, she left what she loved most—for the joy of the return.

This special absence had been a thrilling experience. During the first six months of exile, she had been excited by the novelty of living in semi-royal surroundings. Everything was so exaggerated and unreal that she had a confused sense of having strayed into some fairy tale. She wandered and lost herself amid a maze of pillared halls and gilded apartments. There seemed to be endless marble stairs—countless galleries—all duplicated in enormous mirrors, so that at least one-half of the castle was illusion.

The scenery, in its breathless beauty, held the same

bewildering quality of unreality. In her letters to her family she gave up the attempt to describe blue and purple mountains, whose white crests smashed through the sky—boiling jade rivers—lush green valleys—towering precipices.

"There aren't enough adjectives," she wrote. "But it's all simply topping."

True to schedule, however, when she cracked her seventh month of absence, her rapture suffered its first eclipse and she began to realise the drawbacks of living in a castle. To begin with she got lost no longer, and there were not so many marble staircases, since she had located the mirrors.

There were other unpleasant details, including fleas in the thick carpets and rich upholstery, for the hounds were many and the servants few.

Her vast bedroom, which was like a stage royal apartment, was comfortless and cold, since the enormous coloured porcelain stove—resembling a cathedral altarpiece—was insufficiently stoked.

There were ten courses for dinner—but only one knife and fork, which the diner cleaned with bread.

All the men were handsome and respectful, but none seemed to realise that she was a curly-headed girl whose pet sport was refusing curates.

Before her last five months were up she became so homesick that her longing for a small stone house—backed by an apple orchard, and overlooking a country churchyard—grew to a passion. Sick of the theatrical scenery, she would have exchanged all the mountains and rivers for one corner of an English meadow with a clump of elms and a duck-pond.

The night before her return her excitement was so great that she could not sleep, in anticipation of her journey. She could not believe in it, although her luggage was packed and labelled. One suitcase held soiled linen, destined for a real good boil. She did her personal washing in the bathroom, by stealth, since she had seen too many pails emptied into the beautiful green river which was the communal laundry.

As she lay and tossed she heard the faint scream of an engine, muted by distance to an amplified mosquito-ping. It was the night express, which—when farther down the valley—woke up the homesick sleepers in the hotel and whistled their thoughts after it, as though it were a monstrous metallic Pied Piper.

Just as, later, it called to Iris, it now drew the little spinster from her bed. She ran to the window and was in time to see it shoot past the end of the gorge, like a golden rod of light slipping into grooves of darkness.

"To-morrow night *I* shall be in an express, too," she gloated.

It was a rapture to anticipate her long journey, stage by stage and frontier by frontier, until she reached a small dingy station which was merely a halt built amid empty fields. No one would meet her there, because her father was afraid that blundering Sock, in his ecstasy, might leap at the engine and try to lick its face too.

But they would be waiting for her farther down the lane—and her eyes grew misty at the thought of that meeting. Yet even then she would not reach her journey's end until she ran through a dim white gate and a starlit garden, to see the light streaming through an open door.

"Mater," said Miss Froy, with a lump in her throat.

Then a sudden fear touched her heart.

"I've never been so homesick before," she thought. "Is it a warning? Suppose—suppose something happened—to keep me from getting home."

Something happened—something so monstrous and unexpected that she could not really believe in it. It was an adventure which could only be credited in connection with anyone else.

At first she was certain that someone would soon come to her aid. She told herself it was a fortunate circumstance that she had met the charming English girl. They were compatriots, and she could rely on her with utmost confidence, because—were the situation reversed —she knew she would tear the train apart, wheel by wheel, in order to find her.

But as the time crawled on and nothing happened, doubts began to flock into her mind. She remembered that the girl had a touch of sunstroke and was far from well. She might be worse, or even seriously ill. Besides it would be difficult to try to explain the circumstances when one was ignorant of the language.

There was an even worse possibility. Iris might have tried to intervene and been snatched up, too, in the great machine which had caught her up in one of its revolutions. At the thought, Miss Froy's lip grew beaded from desperation and fear.

Then, suddenly, she felt the braking of the train. Its

clatter and roar died down to a grinding slither, and with a mighty jerk the engine stopped.

"They've missed me," she thought triumphantly. "Now they are going to search the train."

And once again she saw the lights of home streaming through the open door.

As she waited in happy expectation she would have been surprised and gratified to know that the beautiful bride—who looked like a film star—was thinking of her.

Although she was only a pawn, she was the central figure in a plot to restore her liberty. At that moment the Professor was standing in the corridor just outside Mrs. Laura's coupé. She had only to call to him and Miss Froy's ultimate release would be put in train.

As there was plenty of time before Trieste was reached, she delayed in order to be quite certain of the wisdom of her decision. Once she had applied the match she could not stop the blaze of publicity.

In reality, however, her mind was made up. Although she had discovered the barrister's drawbacks he was the original prize for which she had played. When she was Lady Brown, Sir Peveril would be merely a husband and she knew how to deal with this useful domestic animal. Hitherto she had been humiliated by the knowledge that his programme did not include marriage, and, in her anxiety to impress him favourably, she had developed an inferiority complex.

Royal smashing tactics suited her better. Her voice was arrogant as she spoke to the barrister.

"What are we stopping for?" she asked, looking out

at a squalid platform, dimly visible in a few flickering lights.

"Frontier," explained the barrister.

"Help! Have we got to get out and go through the Customs?"

"No, we take on the officials here. . . . What's that shock-headed lunatic up to?"

The barrister frowned as Hare raced into the telegraph office, shouting back the while to the guard, who was yelling to him. It was evidently a first-class slanging match, but unintelligible to the English passengers, who were deprived of its finer points.

As a matter of fact it had struck the bright young man that he could save his own valuable time at Trieste if he took advantage of the halt to send off Mrs. Barnes' telegram to Bath, England. The idea, however, did not make him popular with his compatriots.

"Fool's holding us up," growled the barrister, looking at his watch.

To his surprise Laura was perfectly calm at the menace to their time-table.

"Does it matter?" she drawled. "We shall get there."

"We might lose our connection. We've cut it pretty fine. That reminds me of something. I was wondering whether, in *your* interests, we had better part before we get into Italy. We might run up against someone we know."

"Personally I should not compare Italy with Piccadilly Circus. Still, it's on the map. What do you want to do?"

"I could take the Trieste-Paris express. Could you manage by yourself at Milan?"

"Perfectly. I shall find some one. Or some one will find me. In any case, I can look after myself."

There was a confident note in her voice—associated with the dismissal of cooks—for the Professor had just gone back to his compartment. She rose from her seat, prepared to follow him, when the Customs officials appeared at the end of the corridor.

That check was of vital importance to Miss Froy. As Laura did not wish to be interrupted, she waited for the Professor's luggage to be examined. In the interval the barrister had sensed a situation which prompted a few leading questions.

"What makes you look so serious?" he asked.

"You forget, this may be serious for me."

"In what way? We're not parting for ever, are we? I can meet you in London."

"How nice!"

Now that her pride was no longer a buffer between the natural woman and self-expression, Laura felt mistress of the situation. She held the winning card.

"I'm wondering," she said, "if I can endure the name of 'Brown,' after being Mrs. Parmiter."

"Will the occasion arise?"

"Well, if there's a divorce, you could hardly let me down. It's not done, is it, darling?"

"But, my sweet, there will be no divorce."

"I'm not so sure. I know you made it very plain to me that you would not give your wife the evidence to divorce you. But she'll read about us in the papers—and no woman would stand for that."

"You seem very sure of your publicity. Perhaps you have a better knowledge of the possibilities than I have?"

The barrister glowered at her as though she were a hostile witness, for he had realised the threat which underlay her smiles.

She meant to try to rush a situation.

"I can reassure you on one point," he said coldly. "If your husband brings an action, you may lose your own charming name. But you will not be called upon to make the greater sacrifice. There is already one Lady Brown. . . . My wife will never divorce me."

Laura stared at him incredulously.

"You mean, she'd take it lying down?" she asked.

"Does the posture matter? The point is that we have a complete understanding. It would be against our mutual interests ever to part company. . . . But I think there is no real risk of publicity. Do you?"

He knew he had won and she knew it too. His cool level voice stirred up Laura's smouldering passion.

"If there was," she said, "it seems as if I was the only one that stood to lose. You boast that your wife won't divorce you. Well, my husband would. And I thank God for it. At least I am married to a real man with decent natural feelings."

The barrister screwed his monocle in his eye in an instinctive effort to preserve his dignity.

"I'm afraid I've disappointed you," he said. "I had no idea that I had led you to hope for anything beyond a pleasant and unconventional holiday."

Before Laura could speak, the Customs officer entered their compartment and was very courteous and obliging over the luggage and passport of the distinguished Englishman and his beautiful bride.

After he had gone the Professor appeared again in the corridor—still puffing at his pipe.

Laura shivered at the sight of him because he reminded her of what she had nearly lost by a premature disclosure. Her fine house, her social position, her respectability, and perhaps even her children would all have been swept away for a man who would not marry her.

"Thanks be, I sounded him first," she told herself.

Her gain was Miss Froy's loss. The express carried a ghost-passenger, whose passport—although in order—was never examined. An experienced traveller, she realised what had actually happened when the train began to move slowly for the second time.

"Frontier," she thought.

But in the interval between picking up the Customs officials and dropping them again, she swept through a cycle of emotions, as she shot up from midnight to sunshine, and then—through the gradual twilight of suspense, deferred hope and anxiety—sank back again into darkness.

The train rushed on.

CHAPTER XXV

"STRANGE DISAPPEARANCE"

After the Professor had left her Iris slumped down in her seat and listened to the choppy current of the train's frantic rhythm. The grimed glass was beginning to grow steamy, so that it was difficult to see anything outside the window, except an occasional line of lights when the express flashed through some small station.

Since Miss Froy had been proved non-existent by the laws of logic she felt too flat to be interested in her surroundings. She had not even sufficient spirit to remain angry with the Professor for his interference.

"All travellers are selfish," she reflected. "It was those Miss Flood-Porters. They were afraid they might be saddled with me, so they got at the Professor. I expect he consulted the doctor about what could be done."

She straightened herself in an effort to relieve the aching of her back. The continual shaking of the train had worn her out, while her neck felt as though it were made of plaster of Paris and would crack in two if she jerked it. At that moment she longed for a comfortable bed where she could rest, far from the incessant rattle and din.

It was the doctor's suggestion—a good night's rest. Yet, although she began to doubt her own wisdom in trying to swim against the current, she remained set in her determination to oppose advice.

Presently Hare entered and sat opposite to her in

Frau Kummer's seat. "Well?" he asked hopefully. "Going to stop off at Trieste?"

"No," replied Iris stiffly.

"But are you sure you're fit to go on?"

"Does it matter to you?"

"No. But, all the same, I'm worried stiff about you."

"Why?"

"Hanged if I know. It's not a habit of mine."

Against her will Iris smiled faintly. She could not forget Miss Froy. The memory of her was a grumbling undercurrent, like the aching of a stopped tooth. Yet whenever Hare was present he acted in the same manner as a local application that deadened the pain. In spite of her misery there was a queer thrill in being alone with him on the same nightmare journey.

"Cheer up," he said. "You'll soon be home. Back with your colony of friends."

The prospect seemed suddenly distasteful to Iris.

"I don't want to see one of them," she declared petulantly. "I don't want to get back. I've no home. And nothing seems worth while."

"What do you do with yourself?"

"Nothing. . . . Oh, play about."

"With other chaps?"

"Yes. We all do the same things. Silly things. There's not one real person among the lot of us. . . . Sometimes I get terrified. I'm wasting my youth. What's at the end of it all?"

Hare made no attempt to console her or answer her question. He stared out at the darkness with a half-smile playing round his mouth. When he began to talk, it was about himself.

"My life's very different from yours. I never know where I'm going next. But it's always rough. And things happen. Not always pleasant things. . . . Still, if I could take you with me on my next job, you'd get a complete change. You'd go without every comfort a refined home should have—but I'd lay you odds you'd never feel bored again."

"Sounds lovely. . . . Are you proposing to me?"

"No. Just waiting to dodge when you start to throw custard pies at me."

"But lots of men propose to me. And I'd like to go to a rough place."

"Fine. Now I can go into it seriously. Got any money?"

"Some. Just chicken feed."

"Suits me. I've none."

They were scarcely conscious of what they said as they talked at random in the only language they knew—their light words utterly at variance with the yearning in their eyes.

"You know," said Hare, breaking a pause, "all this is rot. I'm only doing it to take your mind off things."

"You mean—Miss Froy?"

"Yes, confound the woman."

To his surprise Iris changed the subject.

"What sort of brain have you?" she asked.

"Fair to middling, when it's lubricated. It works best on beer."

"Could you write a detective thriller?"

"No. Can't spell."

"But could you solve one?"

"Every time."

"Then suppose you give me a demonstration. You've been very clever in proving Miss Froy could not exist. But—if she did—could you find out what *might* have happened to her? Or is it too difficult?"

Hare burst out laughing.

"I used to think," he said, "that if ever I liked a girl, I'd be cut out by some beautiful band conductor with waved hair. I'm hanged if I thought I'd have to play second fiddle to an ancient governess. Time's revenge, I suppose. Long ago, I bit one. And she was a good governess. . . . Well, here goes."

He lit his pipe and furrowed his brow while Iris watched him with intense interest. His face—no longer slack and careless—was hardened into lines of concentration, so that he looked almost a different man. Sometimes he ran his fingers through his hair, when his rebellious tuft flared up rampant and sometimes he chuckled.

Presently he gave a crow of triumph. "I've got it to fit. Bit of jiggery-pokery in parts, but it hangs together. Now would you like to hear an original story called 'The Strange Disappearance of Miss Froy'?"

Iris winced at the light tone.

"I'd love to," she told him.

"Then you're for it. But, first of all, when you boarded the train, was there one nun next door to you, or two?"

"I only noticed one as we passed the carriage. She had a horrible face."

"Hum. My story demands a second one, later on."

"That's convenient, because there is another one. I met her in the corridor."

"Seen her since?"

"No, but I shouldn't notice one way or another. There's such a jam."

"Good. That proves that no one would be likely to notice whether there was one nun, or two, connected with the invalid outfit. Especially as it's corked up at the end of the corridor. You see, I've got to play about with these blessed nuns, so they're very important."

"Yes. Go on."

"I haven't started yet. The nun part was preamble. Here really goes. . . . Miss Froy is a spy who's got some information which she's sneaking out of the country. So she's got to be bumped off. And what better way than on a railway journey?"

"You mean—they've thrown her on the rails going through a tunnel?" asked Iris faintly.

"Don't be absurd. And don't look so wan. If they chucked her on the line her body would be found and awkward questions asked. No, she's got to *disappear*. And what I was getting at was this. On a journey, a lot of valuable time will be wasted before it can be proved even that she is missing. At first her people will think she's lost a connection or stopped at Paris for a day or two, to shop. So, by the time they get busy, the trail will be stone cold."

"But they wouldn't know what to do. They're old and helpless."

"Tough luck. You're making my tale positively pathetic. But even if they are influential and know the ropes, when they begin to make inquiries they'd find themselves up against a conspiracy of silence."

"Why, is the whole train in the plot?"

"No, just the Baroness, the doctor and the nuns. Of course, there'd be a passive conspiracy of silence, as I mentioned before. None of the passengers, who are local folk, would dare to contradict any statement of the Baroness."

"But, don't forget the Baroness said something to the ticket-collector which you couldn't understand."

"Is this my yarn or yours? But—perhaps you're right. There may be a railway official or two in it. In fact, there must have been some dirty work at the cross-roads over her reserved seat. They had to be sure that she would be in the Baroness' compartment, and at the end of the train."

"Next door to the doctor, too. . . . But what's *happened* to her?"

In spite of her resolution to keep cool, Iris clenched her fingers in suspense as she waited.

"Aha," gloated Hare. "That's where my brain comes in. . . . Miss Froy is lying in the next compartment to this, covered with rugs, and disguised with bandages and trimmings. Her own mother wouldn't know her now."

"How? When?"

"It happened when you obligingly dropped off to sleep. Enter the doctor. He asks Miss Froy if she could render some slight service to his patient. I'm sure I don't know why he should rope her in as he's got a nurse on tap. But she'll go."

"I know she would."

"Well, directly she enters the compartment she gets the surprise of her life. To begin with all the blinds are drawn down and the place is in darkness. She smells a rat, but before she can squeal the three of them set on her."

"The three?"

"*Fa*, the patient is one of the gang. One of them pinions her, the other throttles her so she can't shout, and the doctor is busy giving her an injection, to make her unconscious."

Iris felt her heart hammer as she pictured the scene.

"It *could* happen," she said.

Hare gave her a delighted beam.

"Wish I had you to listen to my golf-stories. You've got the right reaction to lies. Artistic ones, of course. . . . By the way, one of the nuns is a man. The one with the ugly face."

"I believe she is."

"Don't be so prejudiced. All men aren't ugly. Well, Miss Froy is now down and out, so they're able to bandage her up roughly, and stick a lot of plaster over her face, to disguise her. Then they tie her up, gag her, and lay her out, in the place of the false patient, who was already dressed in uniform, only she was covered with rugs. So she's only to pull off her plaster and stick a veil over her bandaged head, to look the perfect nun. Number two."

"I saw a second one in the corridor," nodded Iris.

"But, by now, you've unearthed some English people who will remember Miss Froy, and you've roped in the parson's wife. As I think I explained before, the conspirators have to produce some one, and trust to bluff. So, down comes the blind again, while the second nun—the one who posed as the original patient, dresses herself in Miss Froy's clothes."

As Iris remained silent Hare looked rather depressed.

"Admittedly feeble," he said, "but the best I can do."

Iris scarcely heard him, for she was nerving herself to ask a question.

"What will happen to her when they reach Trieste?"

"Oh, this is the part my readers will adore," explained Hare. "She'll be put in an ambulance and taken to some lonely house, overlooking deep deserted water—a creek, or arm of the river, or something. You know the sort of thing—black oily water lapping a derelict quay. Then she'll be weighted, and all that, and neatly dumped among the mud and ooze. But I'm not altogether ruthless. I'll let them keep her drugged to the bitter end. So the old dear'll know nothing about it. . . . Here. What's up?"

Iris had sprung to her feet and was tugging at the door.

"Everything you say *may* be true," she panted. "We mustn't waste time. We must do something."

Hare forced her back to her seat.

"Here—*you*," he said. Already she meant everything to him but he'd completely forgotten her name. "This is simply a yarn I made up for you."

"But I must get to that patient," cried Iris. "It's Miss Froy. I must see for myself."

"Don't be a fool. The patient next door is *real*, and she's been smashed up. If we forced our way into that carriage and started to make any fuss the doctor would order us out. And quite right too."

"Then you won't help me?" asked Iris despairingly.

"Definitely no. I'm sorry to keep harping on it, but I can't forget your sunstroke. And when I remember my own experience and how I mistook my own footer captain—"

"For the Prince of Wales. I know, I know."

"I'm frightfully sorry I led you on. I only told you how things *might* be worked. But I'm just like the old lady who saw a giraffe for the first time. Honestly, '*I don't believe it.*'"

CHAPTER XXVI

SIGNATURE

"Of course," agreed Iris dully, "you were just making it up. What a fool I am!"

As she tried to stifle her disappointment some one—farther down the corridor—began to speak in a un-naturally loud voice. The words were unintelligible to her and sounded like an incantation for rain; but Hare's face lit up. "Some one's got a wireless set," he said springing up. "It's the news. Back in two shakes."

When he returned he told Iris what he had heard.

"Another good murder sensation gone west. The medical evidence on the editor states he was shot about midnight—while the High Hat had left for his hunting-lodge directly after dinner. So they can't hang it on him. Pity."

As he spoke something floated across Iris' memory, like one of those spirals of cobweb which are wafted on the air on still autumn mornings. She started up as Hare looked at his watch.

"Nearly time for the second dinner," he told her. "Coming?"

"No. But the others will be coming back."

"What's the odds? Are you frightened of them?"

"Don't be absurd. But they make a little clump, all together, this end. And I—I don't like being so near that doctor."

"*Not* frightened then. Well, our compartment will be

empty while the Professor and I are having dinner. I am willing to sub-let it, at a nominal rent, to a good tenant."

After he had gone Iris felt the old limpness stealing over her. A long-drawn howl, as though some damned soul were lamenting, followed by the rattle of machine-gun fire, told her that they were passing through a tunnel. It suggested a gruesome possibility.

Suppose—at that minute—a dead body were being thrown out of the train.

She reminded herself that Hare's story was fiction and managed to drive it from her mind. But another tale—which she had read in a magazine and which was supposed to be authentic—slipped in to take its place.

It was about two ladies who arrived by night at a Continental hotel, on their way back from an Oriental tour. The daughter carefully noted the number of her mother's room before she went to her own. When she returned some time later, she found no trace of her mother, while the room itself had different furniture and a new wallpaper.

When she made inquiries, the entire staff, from the manager downwards, assured her that she had come to the hotel alone. The mother's name was not in the register. The cab-driver and the porters at the railway terminus all supported the conspiracy.

The mother had been blown out like a match.

Of course there was an explanation. In the daughter's absence the mother had died of plague, contracted in the East. The mere rumour would have kept away millions of visitors from the exhibition about to be held in the city. With such important interests at stake a unit had to be sacrificed.

Iris' hands began to grow clammy as she wondered whether Miss Froy's disappearance might not be a parallel on a very small scale. In her case it would not involve a vast and complicated organisation, or a fantastic conspiracy—merely the collusion of a few interested persons.

And Hare had shown her how it *could* be worked.

She began to try to fit the facts to the theory. To begin with, although the Baroness was wealthy, she was sharing a compartment with the proletariat. Why? Because she had decided to take her journey at the last minute and was unable to make a reservation? In that case, the Flood-Porters and the Todhunters could not have secured coupés.

Then was it meanness? Or was it because she wanted a special compartment at the end of the corridor, next to the doctor's carriage, where they would not be seen nor disturbed?

Further—was it chance that the rest of the seats were occupied by local people whose destinies she swayed to a great extent?

The questions hung in the air while a cloud of fresh suspicions quivered into Iris' mind. It was an extraordinary fact that the blinds remained undrawn in the invalid's compartment. She was left on show—so to speak—to declare the goods. Was that to prepare the way for a version of the old strategy—to hide an object in some place where it was visible to every one?

Only—what had poor little Miss Froy done? Hare

was right when he declared that he was influenced mainly by the question of motive. As far as Iris could tell she had discharged her duties so faithfully that her august employer had personally thanked her for services rendered.

Suddenly Iris caught her breath with excitement.

"That was *why*," she whispered.

The personage was supposed to be in his hunting-lodge at the time of the murder. Yet Miss Froy, by tactlessly lying awake, had surprised him coming from the one and only bathroom, where presumably he had been washing before he flitted.

She had destroyed his alibi.

Her knowledge would be a positive danger in view of the fact that she was returning to teach the children of the Red leader. Every one knew that she was a confirmed gossip and rattle. She would be proud of the personage's confidence and advertise it. And, as a British subject—with no axe to grind—her testimony would have weight against a mass of interested evidence.

When the personage shook hands so graciously with her, he was sealing her doom.

Iris pictured the hurried family conference at dawn —the hasty summons to the necessary confederates. Telephones would be humming with secret messages. In view of the urgency, it followed of necessity that Miss Froy's suppression could not be the perfect crime.

She tried to control the gallop of her imagination.

"Maximilian-Max"—she had not forgotten his name, since "Hare was too long"—"spun me a yarn. He was stretching the facts to make them fit in. Perhaps I'm doing the same. It's futile to palpitate about some one who may not exist. After all, as they say, she may be only a delusion. . . . I do wish I could be sure."

Her wish was granted in a dramatic manner. The carriage had grown hot and the steam on the window was turning gradually to beads of moisture, which were beginning to trickle downwards.

Iris followed the slow slide of one of these drops from the top down to a grimy corner of uncleaned pane.

Suddenly she gave a start as she noticed a tiny name which had been written on the smoked glass.

Leaning over she was able to decipher the signature. It was "Winifred Froy."

CHAPTER XXVII

THE ACID TEST

Iris stared at the name, hardly able to believe that her eyes were not playing her a trick. The tiny neat handwriting was round and unformed as that of a schoolgirl, and suggested the character of the little governess—half-prim adult, and half-arrested youth.

It was proof positive that Miss Froy had sat recently in the corner seat. Iris vaguely remembered that she was knitting when she first entered the carriage. When she scrawled her name on the grimy glass with the point of one of her pins, she was working off some of the gush of her holiday mood.

"I was right, after all," thought Iris exultantly.

It was an overwhelming relief to emerge from the fog of her nightmare. But her exhilaration was blotted out almost immediately by a sense of impending crisis.

She was no longer fighting shadows—but facing actual danger.

A terrible fate awaited Miss Froy. She was the only person on the train who realised the peril. And time was slipping remorselessly away. A glance at her watch showed that it was ten minutes past nine. In less than an hour they would arrive at Trieste.

Trieste now assumed a terrible significance. It was the place of execution.

The train was rushing at tremendous speed, in a drive to make up lost time. It rattled and shrieked as it swung round the curves—shaking the carriages as though it recked nothing of its human load. Iris felt that they were in the grip of an insensate maddened force, which, itself, was a victim to a relentless system.

The driver would be fined for every minute over the scheduled time of arrival.

The sense of urgency made Iris spring up from her seat, only to stagger back again at a sudden wave of faintness. She felt a knocking inside her head and stabbing pains behind her eyeballs, as the result of her unguarded movement. With a vague hope that it might act as an opiate she lit a cigarette.

A babel of voices in the corridor told her that the passengers were returning from dinner. The family party, with the blonde, came first. They were all in excellent spirits after their meal and took no notice of Iris, who glowered at them from her corner. She resented their passive conspiracy, even although they were ignorant of any threat to Miss Froy, and were pleased only to be of some slight service to the Baroness.

They were followed by the woman who wore Miss Froy's tweed suit and feathered hat. At the sight of the impostor, Iris' temperature rushed up again as she asked herself whether this were actually the second nursing-sister whom she had met in the corridor.

Both had dull black eyes, a sallow skin, and bad teeth; but the peasants in the railway waiting-room had looked much the same. As it was impossible to reach any conclusion, Iris rose and dashed out into the corridor.

She was strung up to action and intended to storm the next carriage. But blocking her way and almost filling the narrow space was the gigantic black figure of the Baroness. As she towered above her, Iris realised that she was bottled up in the danger-zone of the train—away from every one she knew.

She felt suddenly helpless and afraid as she looked away from the grim face to the shrieking darkness rushing past the window. The maniac shrieks of the engine and the frantic shaking of the train increased her sense of nightmare. Once again her knees began to shake and she had a terrible fear that she was going to faint.

Her horror of becoming insensible and so being at their mercy made her fight the dizziness with every ounce of her strength. Licking her dry lips, she managed to speak to the Baroness.

"Let me pass, please."

Instead of giving way, the Baroness looked at her twitching face.

"You are in pain," she said. "That is not good, for you are young and you travel without friends. I will ask the nurse here for a tablet to relieve your head."

"No, thank you," said Iris firmly. "Please, will you stand on one side?"

The Baroness took no notice of her request, or of her refusal. Instead, she shouted some imperative command which brought the callous-faced nurse to the doorway of the invalid's carriage. Iris noticed sub-consciously that the Baroness' words did not conform to a conventional request, but were a peremptory order for prompt action.

The glass of the patient's window was also growing steamy from heat, but Iris tried to look inside. The still form laid out on the seat appeared to have no face—only a white blur.

As she asked herself what lay underneath the bandages, the nurse noticed her interest. She pounced forward and gripped the girl's arm, as though to pull her inside.

Iris looked up at the brutal mouth, the dark shading round the lips and the muscular fingers, which were covered with short black hairs.

"It *is* a man," she thought.

Terror urged her to an elemental action of self-defence. She was scarcely conscious of what she did as she pressed the end of her smouldering cigarette against the back of the woman's hand. Taken by surprise, she relaxed her grip with what sounded like an oath.

In that instant Iris pushed past the Baroness and dashed down the corridor, fighting her way against the stream of returning diners. Although they opposed her advance, she was glad of their presence, because they formed a barrier between her and the Baroness.

As her terror waned, she began to realise that every one in the train seemed to be laughing at her. The guard openly sneered as he twisted his little black spiked moustache. There was a white flash of teeth and hoots of smothered laughter. The passengers evidently considered her slightly mad and were amused by a funny spectacle.

Their derision made Iris aware of the situation. She felt self-conscious and ashamed as though she were in an unclothed kind of dream.

"Heavens, what have I done?" she asked herself.

"That nurse only offered me some aspirin, or something. And I burned her wrist. If they're really on the level, they will think me mad."

Then her terror flared up again at the thought of Miss Froy.

"They won't listen to me. But I *must* make them understand about her. . . . This train seems a mile long. I'll never get there. . . . Faces. Grinning faces. . . . Miss Froy. It must be in time."

She seemed imprisoned in some horrible nightmare, where her limbs were weighted with lead and refused to obey her will. The passengers blocked her way, so that she appeared to recede two steps where she advanced one. To her distorted imagination, the faces of these strangers were caricatures of humanity—blank, insensible and heartless. While Miss Froy was going to be murdered, no one cared for anything but dinner.

After an age-long struggle through several sections of the train—when the connecting-passages turned to clanking iron concertinas, which tried to catch her and press her to death—she reached the restaurant-car. As she heard the clink of china and the hum of voices, her brain-storm passed and she lingered in the entrance—her returning sense of convention at war with elemental fear and horror.

Soup was being served, and the diners were spooning it up vigorously, for they had been waiting a long time for their meal. In her lucid interval, Iris realised the hopeless prospect of trying to convince hungry men who had only just begun their dinner.

Once again she ran the gauntlet of faces as she reeled

down the gangway. Two waiters, whispering to one another, tittered, and she felt sure that they were sneering at her.

The Professor, who shared a table with Hare, saw her first, and an expression of apprehension flitted across his long face. He was chatting to the doctor, who had lingered over his coffee and liqueur, since the places for the second dinner were not all filled.

Iris felt chilled by her reception when they all stared at her in silence. Even Hare's eyes held no welcome, as he watched her with a worried frown.

In desperation she appealed to the Professor.

"For heaven's sake go on with your soup. Don't stop—but please listen. This is of deadly importance. I know there *is* a Miss Froy. I know there's a conspiracy against her. And I know *why*."

The Professor gave a resigned shrug as he continued drinking his soup. As Iris poured out her incoherent story, she was herself appalled by the weakness of her arguments. Before she finished she despaired of convincing him. He listened in stony silence, and was obviously absorbed by the exact proportion of salt to add to his soup.

At the end of the tale he raised his brows interrogatively as he glanced at the doctor, who broke into some rapid explanation. Watching their faces with anxious eyes, Iris could tell that Hare was disturbed by what was said, for he cut into the conversation.

"That's not her yarn. It's mine. I spun it for a lark, and the poor kid sucked it in. So, if anyone's loopy, it's—"

He broke off, suddenly aware of what he had revealed. But Iris was too distraught to notice implications.

"Won't you come now?" she entreated the Professor.

He looked at his empty plate which the waiter had placed in readiness for the fish course.

"Can't it wait until after dinner?" he asked wearily.

"*Wait?* Won't you understand. It's deadly, terribly urgent. When we reach Trieste it will be too late."

Again the Professor mutely consulted the doctor, who stared fixedly at Iris as though he were trying to hypnotise her. When at last he spoke, it was in English for her benefit.

"Perhaps we had better come at once to see my patient. I'm sorry that your dinner should be spoiled, Professor. But the young lady is in a very highly-strung condition. It may be—safer—to try and reassure her."

Wearing the expression of a martyr to his sense of justice, the Professor unfolded himself from his seat. Once again the little procession staggered in single file down the corridors of the reeling train. As they neared the end, Hare turned and spoke to Iris in a fierce whisper.

"Don't be a blasted fool and start anything."

Her heart sank as she realised that his advice was too late. The nursing-sister was already displaying her hand for the benefit of the doctor and the Professor. Iris noticed vaguely that she had wound a handkerchief around her wrist as though she wished to conceal it from too close a scrutiny.

Then the doctor turned to her and spoke in soothing-syrupy accents.

"My dear young lady, wasn't it rather—impetuous—to burn my poor nurse? And all because she offered you a harmless tablet to relieve the pain of your head. . . . See, Professor, how her face twitches."

Iris shrank as he touched her forehead with a cold forefinger to illustrate his meaning.

Suddenly she remembered that when one is losing a defensive game, the only hope is to attack. Plucking up her courage, she managed to steady her voice.

"I cannot be sorry enough about the burn. It's no excuse to say I was hysterical. But there was some excuse for my being so. There is so much that I cannot understand."

The doctor accepted her challenge.

"Such as—?" he asked.

"Well, the Professor tells me you offered to take me to a nursing home at Trieste."

"The offer is still open."

"Yet you are supposed to be rushing a patient to hospital for a dangerous operation. How could you possibly bother yourself with a complete stranger?. . . It makes one wonder exactly how serious her injuries are. Or if she has any at all."

The doctor stroked his beard.

"My offer was made merely to relieve the Professor of an unwelcome responsibility, which is in my line and not in his. But I am afraid that you exaggerate your own importance. My intention was to give you a seat in the ambulance which took us to the hospital. After we had gone inside with our patient, the driver would follow his instructions and drive you to some recommended nursing home. It was not for professional service—but merely to give you a good night's rest, so that you could continue your journey on the following day."

The proposal sounded so reasonable that Iris could only fall back on her second question.

"Where is the other nurse?"

The doctor paused perceptibly before his reply.

"There is only one nurse."

As she looked at his impassive face, further screened by his black spade-beard, Iris knew instinctively that it was useless to protest. The result would be the same—denials on every side. No one but herself would have seen that second nurse. Just as no one would accept Miss Froy's signature as genuine—supposing that it had not been already destroyed by condensation.

The doctor spoke to the Professor.

"I am sorry to detain you further," he said, "but here is a young lady who believes very terrible things. We must try to convince her of her *delusions*."

He crossed to the shrouded form of his patient and pulled up a corner of one of the rugs, displaying a neat pair of legs.

"Can you identify these stockings or these boots?" he asked.

Iris shook her head as she looked at the thick silk stockings and regulation brown calf single-strap shoes.

"You know I can't," she said. "But you might have better luck if you would raise just one bandage and let me see her face."

The doctor grimaced with horror.

"Ah," he said, "I see you do not understand. I must tell you something that is not pretty. Listen." He touched the swathed forehead with a butterfly flick of his fingertips. "There is no face here at all. *No face.* Only lumps of raw flesh. Perhaps we shall make quite another face, if we are lucky. We shall see."

His fingers moved on and hovered for a second over the bandage which covered the eyes of the figure.

"We await the oculist's verdict on these," he said. "Till then, we dare not expose them to a flicker of light. It may be total blindness, for one eye is but pulp. But science can work marvels."

He smiled at Iris and continued.

"But most terrible of all is the injury to the brain. I will not describe it, for already you look sick. First of all we must attend to that. Afterwards—the rest, if the patient still lives."

"I don't believe you," Iris told him. "It's all lies."

"In that case," said the doctor smoothly, "you can convince yourself. You have only to tear one little strip of plaster from the face, to see. . . . But if you do, I warn you that bleeding will start again and the patient will die instantly from shock. . . . You will be charged with murder and you will be hanged. . . . But since you are so sure of the face which is under these bandages, you will not hesitate. . . . *Will* you tear off this strip?"

Iris felt Hare's fingers closing over her arm, as she hesitated. Her instinct told her that the doctor was putting up a bluff, and that she ought to grasp at even the hundredth chance to save Miss Froy's life.

Yet the doctor had done his work too well. The thought of that mutilated face spouting fountains of blood made her shrink back. Afterwards? The rope—or Broadmoor for life. It was too horrible a prospect to contemplate.

"I—I can't," she whispered.

"Ah," sneered the doctor, "you talk, but you are not so brave."

For the first time it struck Iris that he had never intended to risk his patient. Had he done so, he would have committed professional suicide. Both he and the nurse were on guard, to anticipate her movements.

All the same, he had some ulterior object in view, for he seemed disappointed.

At the time Iris was too sick at heart over her own cowardice to question further. She realised that she had two enemies in the carriage.

The doctor—and herself.

CHAPTER XXVIII

RAISE YOUR HAND

Iris started from her daze to realise that the Professor was talking of dinner.

"If you would hurry back to the dining-car, Hare," he said hopefully, "you might explain to the waiter that we've missed the fish course."

"He'd only say it was 'off'," Hare told him. "They've got to rush the second dinner through before we make Trieste."

"Tut, tut." The Professor clicked. "In that case, we had better return at once. Perhaps you would go on ahead and order extra portions of meat, since we've gone without our fish."

"Not their fault. We walked out on the fish. But I'll see what can be done about it."

Hare checked himself and turned to Iris rather doubt-fully.

"Do you mind?" he asked.

She gave an hysterical laugh, for it had just struck her that although the Professor was confident of his ability to conduct her investigation, he would not risk his linguistic talent where vital interests were concerned.

"Go back, for pity's sake," she said. "Nothing matters but dinner, does it?"

The Professor, whose lean face had brightened at the prospect of food, resented her reproach. Although famished, he felt he must defend his own reputation for meticulous justice.

"Are you being quite fair?" he asked. "We've paid a stiff price for a meal, so we are entitled to claim—at least—a portion of it. And you must admit we have not spared time or convenience in trying to convince you of your mistake."

She shook her head, but she was oppressed by a weight of hopelessness. There seemed nothing more to be done to help Miss Froy. Any attempt at interference would only expose her to the risk of reprisal.

It was not cowardice alone that made her fear the power of the doctor, but common sense. Since she was the sole person on the train who believed in Miss Froy's existence, it stood to reason that she could be of use to her only if she were a free agent.

Her one chance lay in convincing the Professor that there was a real need of further investigation. Although she disliked him, he possessed those qualities which counted in such a crisis. He was pig-headed, coolly humane, and rigidly just. If he were morally certain that he was right, nothing could shake him, and he would plug away at his objective in face of all opposition.

It was bad luck that—at the moment—he was con-centrating on his dinner.

Her curdled brain cleared just as he was about to leave the carriage.

"Professor," she said, "if I'm right, when you get back to England you'll read about a missing Englishwoman— Miss Froy. When you do, it will be too late to save her.

Won't it haunt you for the rest of your life, that you wouldn't listen to me *now*?"

"I might regret it," admitted the Professor, "only the occasion is not likely to arise."

"But if you'll only do something—a very little thing—later you won't have to be sorry at all. And you won't have to cut short your dinner."

"What is it that you want me to do?"

"Go with the doctor to the Trieste hospital and watch while a bandage or strip of plaster is removed. Just enough to show you that there is genuine injury."

Although the Professor was staggered by the suggestion, he considered it slowly with habitual conscientiousness. It encouraged Iris to follow up her advantage with a fresh argument.

"You must admit, *I* can do nothing. I'm not a lunatic and it might mean manslaughter. Besides, the doctor wouldn't let me. So it boils down to this. His precious test means nothing at all."

At her words, the first distrust of the doctor entered the Professor's mind. It was visible in his puckered face and drumming fingers. He always counted the cost before he entertained any project, although it was typical of his high sense of duty that it could not deter him.

In this case the drawbacks were numerous, the chief of which was finance. Although he was no spendthrift, his standard of living at Cambridge was only covered by his salary, and he had to encroach on his capital for holidays. To get a complete mental change he went away at least three times a year, so he had to practise economy.

As the most expensive part of this special trip was the long railway journey, he had booked through one of the cheaper tourist agencies which specialised in cut-prices. Therefore, his ticket would not admit his breaking the journey anywhere.

To make matters more difficult he was short of cash, since his dislike of communal travel had made him yield to the temptation of sharing a coupé with Hare on the return journey.

There was another and more urgent reason why he should not stop at Trieste for the night. Delay involved the sacrifice of a cherished engagement. He had been invited to spend the following week-end with an elderly peer—an intellectual recluse—who lived in a remote corner of Wales. If he reached England on Saturday, instead of Friday, it would be too late.

The doctor watched him closely as he frowned and tapped his cheek-bones.

"Is it not convenient for you to stop at Trieste?" he asked.

"Definitely inconvenient."

"I am sorry. Because, in my own interest, I must beg of you to do what this young lady asks."

"Why?" asked the Professor, incensed by this double assault on his week-end.

"Because I am growing convinced that there must be some reason for this poor young lady's distress. It is always 'Miss Froy.' Is that a common name in England, like 'Smith'?"

"It is not familiar to me."

"But she had heard it before—and in connection with

213

some terrible experience. I do not know what has happened. But I *think* that there really is a lady called 'Miss Froy,' and that some harm has happened to her. I think, too, that this poor young lady knew, but the shock has driven away all memory."

"Absurd," interrupted Iris. "I won't—"

"Shut up," whispered Hare fiercely.

He had listened with close attention, for he was beginning to wonder whether the doctor had not found the true explanation of Iris' delusion. She had been unconscious until just before she managed to catch the train. Although the explanation was sunstroke, it might have been supplied through the agency of some interested person, who wanted to confuse her recollection.

"You will understand," went on the doctor, "that I do not wish to be under any suspicion, if—later—a lady might be declared missing."

"It's a preposterous idea," said the Professor. "Besides, the hospital authorities would back you up."

"But how am I to prove that it is *this* patient I bring to them, and not some substitute? But if you, Professor, would accompany me to the hospital and wait for the surgeon's initial examination, there can be no further question. It is your high reputation that I crave for my protection."

The Professor smiled bleakly, for he was very hungry. Although he was an excellent bridge player, he had no knowledge of poker. Consequently the doctor's offer seemed to him proof positive that there was not even the flimsiest foundation for Iris' fantastic theory.

"I think you are carrying professional caution too

far," he said. "Miss Carr"—unlike Hare, he was used to memorising names—"has declared that she went to the dining-car with one lady whom she called 'Miss Froy' —and that lady has since been identified as a Frau Kummer. . . . She is not well, which accounts for her mistake. . . . In the circumstances, there is no shred of evidence that the real Miss Froy—if there is such a person—is on the train at all."

"Then, in case of future trouble, may I apply to you to support any statement I might make?" asked the doctor.

"Certainly. I will give you my card."

The Professor wheeled round and turned dinner-wards.

Hare divined that Iris was on the verge of an explosion. Hitherto he had managed to restrain her by the warning pressure of his hand on her arm, but she was at the end of her patience.

"Don't throw a scene," he implored. "It's no good. Come back to the coop."

Instead of obeying she raised her voice.

"*Miss Froy*. Can you hear me? Hold up your hand if you can."

CHAPTER XXIX

TRIESTE

Miss Froy heard her. She held up her hand.

Although she was blinded by her bandage, she had recognised Iris' voice among a murmur of other sounds. In a confused fashion she realised that people were talking; but their tones were blurred and broken, as though they were far away—giving the impression of an imperfect long-distance call.

She tried to speak to them, but could not because of her gag. Once before she had contrived to move it partially, with frenzied pressure—remembering the while how her father used to tease her about the power of her tongue. She put every ounce of strength into that cry for help, but it was an uncouth, incoherent sound, like an animal in pain.

No one heard her—and her captors had wedged the gag tighter, increasing her discomfort. Her arms were bound to her body above the elbows, and her legs were tied together at the ankles by a surgical bandage. The doctor made no attempt to hide it when he exposed her shoes and stockings for identification. He knew that among such a profusion of strappings one more or less would never be remarked.

However, her hands were free from the wrists, because the supply of bindings had given out, and—in any case—they were powerless to do more than wave feebly. Miss Froy's heart fluttered with joy as she told herself that her clever girl knew that an instantaneous response to her appeal, however slight, would show that the patient recognised her name and was giving proof of identity.

So she spread out her fingers—fan-wise—and flapped them in the air in a pathetic S.O.S.

Then once again her mind, which she was unable to control, slid away. It was cobwebbed and smeared from drugs, but every now and again a corner would clear, like the transparent red stains of juice that veins the scum of boiling jam. In these lucid moments a whirl of memories returned, but in the end her mind always went back to that first moment of shock.

It was incredible—monstrous. She had been sitting in her compartment when the doctor had entered and asked if anyone would help him raise his patient. He explained that the nurse had gone away for a few minutes and the poor creature in his charge had grown restless, as though she were uncomfortable.

It was second-nature to Miss Froy to respond. She was not only always ready to be of service, but she was also anxious to see the crash casualty at closer quarters, besides learning perhaps more about the accident. It would be something with which to thrill the family when she related her adventures on Friday night.

When they entered the patient's compartment the doctor asked her to raise the head while he lifted the body. It was with specially deep sympathy that she bent over the prostrate form, because she was reminded of the contrast between them.

"She's smashed," she thought, "and I'm well and happy. I'm going home."

Suddenly a long pair of white linen-clad arms shot out and clutched her throat.

The helpless patient was gripping her windpipe in a merciless grip. In that appalling moment she remembered a Grand Guignol horror, when an electrified corpse had strangled the man who had galvanised it to synthetic life. Then the pressure tightened, lights flashed under her eyelids, and she knew no more.

For some time the eclipse had been total. Then, gradually there were infinitesimal rifts in the darkness of her senses. She became conscious that she was trussed, gagged and blinded, while muffled voices discussed her fate.

It was not a cheerful prospect. Although she was ignorant of her crime, she had an inkling of her sentence. It was connected with an ambulance which would meet them at Trieste. But it would take her to no hospital.

Yet in spite of cramp and thirst, of bodily anguish and mental torment, she never gave up hope.

It was said in the family that she followed Aunt Jane. In her lifetime, this Victorian lady had wanted a talking-doll, a tricycle, an operatic career, a husband, a legacy. She got none of these things, but she never discarded a single wish, nor doubted that each would be granted—in the end.

When the end came, she was seventy-seven and a pensioner on family charity; yet she closed her eyes with as lively a faith in the talking-doll as in the legacy which would grant her a leisured life and a dignified death.

Aunt Jane helps to explain why Miss Froy remained tolerably calm in the face of each fresh disappointment. Mercifully, however, her clear moments were of brief duration. Most of the time she was in a drugged dream, when she was for ever trying to get home.

She always managed to reach the gate and saw the lighted garden path with its exaggerated hollows—when a displaced pebble revealed a pit. The turf borders and the pink and purple Chinese asters were unnaturally vivid in the lamplight, while the pungent scent of early chrysanthemums hung on the frosty air.

But although she was so near that she could see the cracked red tile in the passage, she knew that something was wrong, and that she would never reach the door. . . . It was when she was struggling out of one of these tantalising visions that she heard Iris calling her name and telling her to hold up her hand.

Unfortunately she did not know that there was a bad block in her system of communication. None of the channels were clear, so that her brain did not register the message from her ears until after the doctor—in a state of indignant horror—had literally swept his visitors out into the corridor. Even after that, some time elapsed before her nerve-centres were linked up with the intelligence department, and by then it was too late.

The blinds had all been drawn down, so there was no one besides the nurse to witness the futile signal of her fluttering fingers.

Outside the door the doctor wiped his face in his agitation.

"That was a terrible thing to do," he said, his voice vibrating with passion. "I was wrong to let you in at all. But I never dreamed you would be so imbecile as to try and injure my poor patient."

As Iris shrank involuntarily before his rage, he appealed to the Professor.

"You can understand, Professor, that absolute quiet is essential for my patient. The grave injury to the head—"

"How can she get quiet on a railway journey?" broke in Iris, as the engine plunged into a tunnel with an ear-splitting yell.

"That is something quite different," explained the doctor. "One can sleep through traffic. It is the slight unaccustomed sound which wakens one from sleep. If she had heard you she might have been called back, while I am doing my utmost—in mercy—to keep her unconscious."

"I quite understand," the Professor assured him. "And I regret this has happened." His voice was glacial as he spoke to Iris. "You had better get back to your carriage, Miss Carr."

"Yes, come on," urged Hare.

Iris felt that they were all against her. In sudden defiance she launched a lone offensive.

"Directly we reach Trieste I am going to the British Embassy," she told them.

They were brave words, but her head was swimming and her knees shook so violently that she felt incapable of carrying out her threat. All the same, her intentions filled her with an illusion of power. Then Hare tackled her in his old international form and carried her along the corridors with the impetus of a tidal-bore, while the Professor plodded in the rear.

"My only hope is we shall get some sort of a dinner," was his parting remark to the doctor.

Iris was too bewildered by what had happened to resist Hare's high-handed treatment. She could not understand why there had been no response to her cry. It shook her confidence and made her feel that her moral cowardice in failing to expose the mystery patient was justified.

Yet even if she were a genuine accident case, the danger which threatened Miss Froy was not dormant. When she was back in the coupé she presented Hare with an ultimatum. "Are you with me or against me? Are you stopping at Trieste?"

"No," replied Hare firmly. "Neither are you."

"I see. Then you didn't mean what you said about liking me—and all that."

"I certainly meant—all that."

"Well, if you don't come with me to the Embassy, I'm through with you."

Hare tugged at his collar miserably.

"Can't you realise I'm your only friend?" he asked.

"If you were a friend you'd prove it."

"Wish I could, only I haven't the spunk. As your best friend, I ought to knock you out, so that you'd stay put for the next twenty-four hours, and rest your poor old head."

"Oh, I hate you," stormed Iris. "Go away!"

In the next compartment the Misses Flood-Porter overheard scraps of the dialogue. "That girl certainly contrives to get some excitement out of a railway journey," remarked the elder sister astringently.

While the young people were quarrelling about her, Miss Froy was lying rigid, with still hands. It had gradually dawned upon her that she had no audience, so her demonstration was wasted. However, she had one crumb of comfort when Iris mentioned appealing to the British Consul. She had heard that cry of defiance through the closed door.

Presently she realised that the hint had not been wasted. There was a low rumbling conference inside the carriage.

"Trieste," remarked a masculine voice. It belonged to the doctor's chauffeur, who was wearing the incongruous uniform of a nursing-sister. "What now?"

"We must waste no time at Trieste," replied the doctor. "We shall have to drive all night, like hell, to get back to protection."

"But—where will you dump the body now?"

The doctor mentioned a place. "It is on our road," he explained. "The wharf is deserted—and the eels swarm."

"Good. They will be hungry. Very soon there will be no face to tell tales, if it should be found later. . . . Will you dump the clothes and baggage there too?"

"Fool. They would be a certain mark of identification there. No, we take them with us in the car. You will incinerate them without delay directly we get back."

Although her brain was so misty, some vibration of

her senses made Miss Froy aware that they were talking about her. She shuddered instinctively at the thought of black stagnant water, thick with mud and scummed with refuse. She had such a violent dislike to corruption.

But she missed the real implication.

The chauffeur went on to anticipate difficulties.

"What if anyone makes inquiries at the Trieste hospitals?"

"We shall explain that the patient died in transit."

"But if they demand to see the corpse?"

"They will see it. There will be no difficulty about that, once we are back. The mortuary will provide me with a female corpse which I will mutilate."

"Hum. I wish I was safely at home. There is still that girl."

"Yes," remarked the doctor, "it is extraordinary how the English will regard themselves as the policemen of the world. Even a girl has the habit. But it is a mistake to think them a stupid nation. That Professor has a good brain, and he is no fool. . . . But luckily, he is honourable, and believes that all the world must be honourable, too. He will support all I say."

"Still, I wish I was back," harped the chauffeur.

"The risk is great," his employer reminded him. "So, also, is the reward."

The drone of masculine voices which drummed against Miss Froy's semi-sealed ears—like the hum of a spinning wheel—ceased. The chauffeur thought of the garage he would buy, while the doctor planned to retire from practice. He did not relish his present commission, but the ruling family claimed his loyalty and self-interest forbade disobedience. Directly the Baroness had sent for him, privately, by night, he had evolved the best scheme he could devise on the spur of the moment, to clear an obstacle in the illustrious pathway.

He knew why he had been chosen, for he, himself, would not use a delicate surgical instrument to cut a tarry string. His reputation was smutted because of recent mishaps at the local hospital. His scientific curiosity was keener than his wish to exterminate disease, and he was under suspicion of having prolonged operations unduly, and at the expense of life.

From the beginning the venture had been unlucky, because of the interference of the English girl. But for her, the little plan would have worked perfectly, by reason of its simplicity, and the small number of confederates. He knew that he and his chauffeur would take their lives in their hands when they scorched home-wards through dangerous passes, rounding dizzy precipices on one wheel, in their effort to race the express back to their native territory.

But once they were back, every emergency would be forestalled. An adequate explanation would be forthcoming to any inquiry. No one would have any awkward knowledge to disclose and every wire that connected the dead patient with Miss Froy would be cut.

"Will you dump the English girl in the sewer, too?" asked the chauffeur suddenly.

"No," replied the doctor. "Further complication would be dangerous. But when we reach Trieste she will not be in a position to make further trouble for us."

Miss Froy heard his words and, for the first time, her

optimism failed her. With a wave of agonised longing she thought of the family at home, for she had sent them her timetable, and she guessed they would be tracing it on the map.

True to her forecast, at that moment they were thinking of her. They had done their best to fight their unusual depression, for they had lighted a fire—composed principally of fir-cones—and had been guilty of an extravagant supper—scrambled eggs. Sock lay on the rug watching the flames. In spite of the welcome warmth, he was still subdued after his disappointment, for he had rushed off against orders to meet the train, with a hope new-born.

Mr. Froy looked at his wife and noticed that the under-lip of her small firm mouth was pendulous and that she sagged in her chair. For the first time he realised that she was his senior, and that he, too, had grown old.

Then he glanced at the clock.

"Winsome's nearly come to the end of her first stage homewards," he told his wife. "She'll soon reach Trieste."

Mrs. Froy passed the information on to the dog.

"Sock, the little mistress is really on her way home now. Every minute she is coming nearer—nearer—nearer. In another half-hour she'll be at Trieste."

Trieste.

CHAPTER XXX

RECANTATION

The waiter managed to salvage some dinner for the Professor and Hare, who ate through the courses in silence. As they were finishing their cheese and biscuits, the doctor entered the dining-car and seated himself at their table.

"I am sorry to disturb you," he said, "but I want a little conference about the young English lady."

The Professor stifled an exclamation, for he feared that Iris had broken out in some fresh indiscretion.

"Coffee, please," he said to the waiter. "Black. . . . Well—what is the trouble *now*?"

"As a medical man I find myself faced with a responsibility," explained the doctor. "The lady is in a dangerous mental state."

"What grounds have you for your conclusion?" asked the Professor, who never accepted a statement without data.

The doctor shrugged.

"Surely it is obvious to the meanest intelligence that she is suffering from a delusion. She invents some one who is not here. But there are other signs. She is highly excitable—suspicious of every one, inclined to be violent—"

As he noticed Hare's involuntary grimace, he broke off and turned to the younger man.

"Pardon. Is the young lady your affianced?"

"No," grunted Hare.

"But perhaps a lover—or a dear friend? Yet it would not surprise me to hear that she has been very angry recently with you. Has she?"

"I'm not really popular at present," admitted Hare.

"Thank you for the confidence, for it confirms my diagnosis. It is always a sign of mental malady when they turn upon those they love best."

He could tell he had captured Hare's sympathy as he continued.

"There is no real danger if we can take a precaution. It is essential at this stage that her brain should be rested. If she could have a long sleep, I am confident she will wake up quite well again. But if we let her persist in working herself up into a fever, the mental mischief may be—irreparable."

"I think there is something in that, Professor," agreed Hare. "It's exactly what I've been thinking myself."

"What do you propose?" asked the Professor cautiously.

"I should suggest," replied the doctor, "that you persuade her to swallow a harmless sedative which I can give you."

"She will object."

"Then it should be given by force."

"Impossible. We cannot control her wishes."

"Then, perhaps, you could trick her into taking it?"

As the Professor remained mulishly silent, the doctor half rose from the table.

"I can assure you," he said, "that I have more than enough responsibility of my own to shoulder, with my patient. I only felt it my duty to warn you. We doctors are pledged to the service of humanity—whether we receive fees or no. But now that I have explained the position, I can leave the decision to you. My own conscience is clear."

The doctor was on the point of departing with dignity when Hare called him back.

"Don't go, doctor. I feel the same as you about this. I've had personal experience of delusions, with concussion." He turned eagerly to the Professor. "Can't we wangle it somehow?"

The Professor's long upper lip seemed to lengthen in his disapproval.

"I could not be a party to such a course," he said. "It would be gross interference with Miss Carr's personal liberty. She is a free agent."

"Then—you'd prefer to remain 'good form' and see her go bughouse?" asked Hare indignantly.

The Professor smiled acidly.

"My own impression is," he told them, "that there is not the slightest danger of that. I have had experience of such cases. My work brings me into contact with neurotic young women. To my mind, Miss Carr is merely hysterical."

"Then—what do you propose?" asked Hare.

"I think a salutary shock will probably bring her to her senses."

Reinforced by his meal, the Professor felt master of the situation. He finished his coffee and liqueur, flicked a crumb from his waistcoat, and rose in a leisurely manner.

"*I* will reason with Miss Carr," he said.

He strolled out of the dining-car and lurched along the corridors. As he passed the coupé occupied by the Misses Flood-Porter, he was tempted to resign his mission and join them in a little chat. The ladies looked so composed and immaculate—for they were well in advance of their preparations for arrival at Trieste—that he was hopeful that further conversation would reveal some mutual friend.

Resolute in his self-imposed duty, he entered his carriage and seated himself opposite to Iris. His first glance told him that she had been lighting cigarette after cigarette, only to throw them away, barely smoked. Although her action was merely a sign of nervous tension, he looked with distaste at the litter of spent matches on the floor and seats.

"Will you take some advice offered in a friendly spirit?" he asked, speaking to her as though she were a fractious child.

"No," replied Iris mutinously, "I want to hear the truth, for a change."

"The truth may be a bit of a shock. But you've asked for it, so you shall have it. . . . The doctor has just told me that, as a result of your sunstroke, you are—very slightly, and only temporarily—deranged."

The Professor honestly believed that he was dealing with a neurotic girl who was telling lies from a love of sensation, so he watched her reaction with complacent confidence. When he saw the horror in her eyes, he felt his experiment was justified.

"Do you mean—*mad*?" she asked in a whisper.

"Oh, dear, no. Nothing to be frightened of. But he is not happy about your safety as you are travelling alone. He may be forced to take steps to ensure it, unless you can manage to keep perfectly quiet."

"What steps?" asked Iris. "Do you mean that nursing home? I should resist. No one can do anything to me against my will."

"In the circumstances, violence would be most unwise. It would only confirm the doctor's fears. But I want to make the position quite clear to you. Listen."

The Professor sawed the air with his forefinger and spoke impressively.

"You have only to keep calm and everything will be all right. No one will interfere with you in any way, unless you remind them of your existence. To be brutally frank, you've made yourself a public nuisance. It's got to stop."

The Professor was not so inhuman as he seemed. His own unpleasant experience with his infatuated student had prejudiced him against emotion, but he thought he was acting in Iris' interests.

Therefore he could have no idea of the hell of fear into which he plunged her. She was white to her lips as she shrank into the corner of the carriage. She was afraid of him—afraid of every one in the train. Even Hare seemed to have entered into the conspiracy against her. The whole world appeared roped into a league that threatened her sanity.

Lighting yet one more cigarette with shaking fingers, she tried to realise the position. It seemed clear that she had blundered into important issues and that, consequently, she had to be suppressed. The Professor had been sent to bribe her with immunity in return for her silence.

Even while she rejected compromise angrily, she had to face the cold truth. She had not a ghost of a chance to fight these influential people. If she persisted in her hopeless quest to find Miss Froy, the doctor would merely pull wires and whisk her away to some nursing home in Trieste.

She remembered Miss Froy's tale of the woman who had been held in a private mental asylum. The same might happen to her. Any opposition on her part would be used as evidence against her sanity. They could keep her imprisoned and under the influence of drugs, until she really crashed under the strain.

It would be some appreciable time before anyone missed her. She was not expected in England, for she had not troubled to engage rooms at an hotel. Her friends would believe that she was still abroad. When at last her lawyers or the bank made inquiries, it would be too late. They would trace her to the nursing home, and arrive to find a lunatic.

In her distraught state, she plunged herself into a morass of distorted fears and exaggerated perils. But although her reason was nearly submerged by a tidal wave of panic, one corner of her brain still functioned on common-sense lines. It convinced her that Miss Froy's rescue was an utterly hopeless proposition.

"Well?" asked the Professor patiently, as she tossed away her unsmoked cigarette.

Suddenly Iris thought of the familiar Calais-Dover

express—the white cliffs—Victoria Station—with almost frantic longing. She felt homesick for England and the cheery casual crowd of her friends. Before her eyes, in letters of fire, flashed the familiar slogan—"SAFETY FIRST."

"Well?" repeated the Professor. "Have you come to your senses?"

Utterly worn out and paralysed with fear, Iris slipped into the trough of lost hopes. She reminded herself that Miss Froy was merely a stranger whom she had tried to help. To persist merely meant a double—and useless—sacrifice. "Yes," she replied dully.

"You'll make no more scenes?" went on the Professor.

"No."

"Good. . . . Now, will you admit to me that you invented Miss Froy?"

Iris felt plunged in the hell of Judas Iscariot and all traitors as she made her denial.

"Yes. I invented her. There's no Miss Froy."

CHAPTER XXXI

A CUP OF SOUP

The doctor looked after the Professor as he went from the dining-car.

"That is a very clever man," he said dryly. "He would cure illness by a scolding. Yet he may be right. Indeed, for the first time in my career, I hope I shall be proved wrong."

He watched Hare's frowning face closely and asked, "What is your opinion?"

"I know he's making a damnable blunder," growled the young man.

"'He that knows, and knows that he knows,'" quoted the doctor, "'he is wise.' . . . Well—what then?"

"Hanged if I know."

"Ah, you feel, perhaps, that the Professor is cleverer than you?"

"I feel nothing of the kind. Our lines are different."

"Then probably you are not used to exert authority?"

"Oh, no. I've only got to control hundreds of toughs—and some of them ready on the draw."

"Then, frankly, I do not understand your hesitation. Unless, of course, you fear the young lady's anger when she discovers she has been tricked. She has what you call 'spirit,' and what I call 'temper,' since I have a very sweet wife myself. . . . Well, it is for you to decide whether you prefer the angry words of a sane woman to the gentle smile of an imbecile."

"Don't rub it in," muttered Hare. "I've got to *think*."

"There is not much time left," the doctor reminded him.

"I know. But—it's the hell of a risk."

"Not at all. Here is my card. I will write a declaration on it that the drug is harmless, under penalty of heavy damages, should the lady be ill afterwards as a direct result. . . . I will do more. You shall have a sample to take back to England, so that you may have it analysed."

Hare pulled at his lip. He knew that the doctor's offer was fair, yet he could not shake off his distrust of the unknown.

The doctor seemed to read his thoughts.

"Perhaps," he said, "you hesitate because I am not Dr. Smith, of London, England. Yet, if you were in a strange city and had a raging toothache, you would seek relief from the first dentist. Remember, a man's name on a brass plate, with certain letters after it, is a profession's guarantee of good faith to the public."

He let the argument sink in while Hare continued to maltreat his face and hair. Presently he glanced at his watch, and then thrust his wrist before the young man's eyes.

"See the time. I must go back to my patient."

Hare sprang up as though galvanised.

"One minute, doctor. How could we give the stuff?"

The doctor knew that the bridge had been crossed as he hastened to explain.

"That poor young lady has had no dinner," he said reproachfully. "Surely you will bring her a small cup of

234

soup, since there will be no opportunities on the Italian train, until they couple the breakfast-car."

"Chump," exclaimed Hare, hitting his head. "I never thought that she'd be hungry. . . . But if she is asleep, how will I manage changing trains at Trieste?"

"Ah, my dear sir, you must not expect miracles. You are too impatient. The drug will not take full effect until she is in the Italian train. Then, she will sleep and sleep. But at Trieste she will merely be very dull, very heavy, very docile. And"—the doctor's eyes narrowed—"she will be far too torpid to worry you about any phantom lady."

"Suits me all right. . . . I'll take a chance."

The doctor accompanied him to the kitchen-car and fought a battle with the protesting chef. In the end medical authority won the day. Not long afterwards, Hare, with anxious eyes and tightly compressed lips, began his fateful journey along the corridors, holding a half-filled bowl.

But he carried so much more than soup. Within the narrow circle of the cup lay the destiny of a woman.

As he staggered on his way—by a coincidence due to the time—in a small stone house in England Mrs. Froy's thoughts turned to nourishment.

"I do hope Winnie will eat something before she gets to Trieste," she said to Mr. Froy. "Her dinner won't stand by her all through the night. Besides she is always too excited to eat on a journey. She merely pecks her first supper at home."

Her husband gave a guilty smile, for he knew the reason for Winnie's lack of appetite.

Meanwhile, Hare was still scared by the responsibility of his step. While he assured himself that he was actually carrying a gift of sanity to Iris, he could not rid himself of apprehension. Tormented by indecision, he proposed a foolish test for himself.

"If I don't spill any it's going to be O.K. But if I do, I'll cry off."

He crabbed slowly along, with utmost care and caution while the train seemed to put on an extra spurt of speed. The soup splashed furiously against the rim of the cup—for ever on the point of brimming over. Yet in some extraordinary manner it always whirled within its confines.

Hare was reminded of a simple circus trick he used to practise—as a boy—with a hoop and a glass of water. Apparently the same principle operated now, and the soup could not be spilt from sheer velocity of motion.

But just before he reached the reserved portion of the train he came to grief completely. As he was crossing the connecting passage, a small boy—rushing from the pursuit of a smaller girl—charged into him and received a baptism of soup, together with an undesirable name.

Hare broke off in his malediction to wipe his fingers.

"That's torn it," he muttered. "Well, it's out of my hands now."

Meanwhile Iris was actually in the grip of a brainstorm. When the Professor left her she was numb with fear. Some vital mainspring in her brain seemed to have snapped, reducing her mind to a limp tangle. Miss Froy was a lost cause—so she denied her. But nothing was left but a void, without aim or hope or self-respect.

"I was her only chance," she told herself. "And now I've crashed too."

The knowledge was torture which she tried vainly to forget. But vivid little thumbnail pictures persisted in flashing before her closed eyes. Two bent old people, huddled in a lighted doorway—waiting. Sock—a woolly blunderbuss—rushing off to meet a mistress who would never come home.

She was most affected by the thought of the dog, for she assumed the senility of the aged parents. She told herself that the shock would probably kill them both, since they would be too devoted—or too used to each other—to survive singly. And then—what would become of the dog, stranded and hungry in a country cottage?

She worked herself into a positive fever about him. As her temperature rose, her head began to ache so furiously that it seemed to bang in a series of small explosions, which kept time with the frantic revolutions of the wheels.

"You're *get*-ting near. You're *get*-ting near."

And then the rhythm changed and began to chop out a devil's tattoo. "Nearer—nearer—nearer—*nearer*—NEARER."

Nearer to Trieste. The express was in the relentless grip of the schedule. The pulsations of the engine throbbed through Iris like the shaking arteries of an overdriven heart. It rocked and roared over the rails—a metal monster racing an invisible rival.

It had to beat Time.

When Hare came into her carriage she hardly raised her eyes, and did not speak to him.

"Still hating me?" he asked.

"I only hate myself," she said dully.

He looked furtively at her twitching face and burning cheeks, which, to his mind, confirmed the doctor's diagnosis of dangerously overstrung nerves, while he assured himself that—since he could not give her that essential sock on the jaw—he was rendering her a real service.

"I've brought you some soup," he said guiltily.

She shrank from it even while she thanked him.

"Sweet of you—but I couldn't touch it."

"Try. It'll make a new man of you."

"All right, then. Leave it, will you?"

"No, that's too old a dodge. The instant I go you'll chuck it out of the window. Well—I'm not going."

Iris clutched her head.

"I feel so sick," she pleaded.

"Lack of nourishment. Listen, my child, there's a history of the try-try-again kind connected with that simple bowl of soup. I slaughtered the chef to get it in the first place. Then, on my way here, some wretched kid bowled the whole lot over. . . . I said, 'Kismet.' And then I said, 'She's had nothing all day and she'll have nothing until to-morrow's breakfast.' And I went all the way back and slaughtered another chef, all to bring you a second cup."

"Oh, well—" sighed Iris helplessly. "But have I got to be grateful?"

She swallowed the first spoonful with reluctance, grimacing as though it were a nauseous draught; then she paused, while Hare waited in acute suspense.

"What *is* it?" she asked. "It's got a horribly druggy taste."

"It's the same soup I wolfed down at dinner. That's all I know," lied Hare.

"Well, I'd better get it over."

Raising the cup to her lips, she gulped it down with a shudder.

"You'll feel better soon," Hare assured her as he took the empty bowl from her nerveless hands.

For some time they sat in silence, while he watched her stealthily, hoping to detect the first sign of drowsiness. He knew that drugs affect people differently, and that it was difficult to gauge the right dose for Iris, because of her abnormal condition.

"If anything goes wrong," he thought desperately, "I'll have to take the rap."

At intervals he heard the whine of the Professor's voice, as he strained it in an effort to be audible above the uproar of the train. He was in the next compartment, improving an acquaintance with the Misses Flood-Porter, which he hoped to authorise with the discovery of a third-party link.

"You live in Somersetshire," he remarked. "It is a county where I have stayed often. I wonder if we know any mutual friends."

"I hate every single person living there," said Miss Rose vehemently, sweeping away any claimants to friendship.

"Stag-hunting," supplemented Miss Flood-Porter.

Relieved by the explanation the Professor began gently and skilfully to extricate a few worthy persons from under the wholesale ban. He was rewarded when the ladies recognised a name.

"Oh, yes. Charming people. Great friends of ours."

The contact was complete and they all shouted against each other.

Iris recognised the voices, for, after a time, she spoke to Hare.

"That's the Professor, isn't it? I wish you'd tell him I want to sleep, but can't, because he's making too much noise. And slip in something about him being a public nuisance, will you? He'd appreciate it. Because that's what he called me."

The speech was so unexpectedly jaunty that Hare stared at her in surprise. He did not know whether he were imagining changes, but her eyes were less strained, while her face seemed to have lost the glazed flush of fever.

"That doctor's sold me a pup," he thought wrathfully. "She is *not* settling down. She's gingering up. At this rate she'll be fighting-mad at Trieste."

As a matter of fact their little conspiracy was hampered by their ignorance of working conditions. On the rare occasions when Iris was unwell, her response to treatment was almost immediate. In her abnormal state she was now beating her own speed record. Although its effects were bound to be short-lived, she was feeling miraculously restored by the nourishment, while the drug was beginning imperceptibly to soothe her brainstorm, like the first film of oil spreading over a rough sea.

She was conscious of a glow of spurious strength, followed by a rush of confidence, as she climbed out of the traitor's hell into which she had hurled herself.

"Lost causes are the only causes worth fighting for," she told herself.

In her relief at her own restoration, she smiled at Hare, who grinned back at her.

"Didn't I tell you you'd feel better after that nice strong good nourishing soup?" he asked.

"It tasted as though it was made from a mummy—but it has picked me up," she admitted. "My head's clearer. I realise now that the Professor was right. I've made an awful fool of myself."

Hare chalked up a good mark to the properties of the drug.

"You mean—you've chucked Miss Froy off the train?" he asked incredulously.

"Please, don't bring her up again. Of course, there's no such person. I told the Professor so."

Iris felt a momentary pang as she looked into his guileless eyes.

"It's a shame to trick him," she thought.

She had resolved on a policy of stratagem. She would sham docility, to avert suspicion. When Trieste was reached, she would contrive to give them the slip and hire a taxi, in which to follow the ambulance. They would not suspect any outside interest in their movements, since she was definitely out of the running.

Having warned the taxi-driver in advance to memorise the address to which Miss Froy was taken, she would drive furiously back to the British Embassy. She had always found Italians gallant and susceptible, so she was sure of enlisting their sympathies and getting immediate action.

Her jammed brain was now clicking on with amazing speed. She told herself that the success of her plan depended on whether she could fool them all. She must return to her own carriage, which was full of the doctor's spies, and sham the requisite limp submission.

"I mustn't overdo it," she thought. "They might want to fuss over me if they thought I was ill."

She counted on the confusion when the passengers, with their luggage, changed trains at the terminus. Hare must be sent off on some errand, since he was her only obstacle. The rest of the travellers would remain true to type and look after their own interests.

She raised her eyes and met Hare's earnest gaze. He was thinking of the nice long sleep which awaited her in the Italian train.

"It's a shame to trick her," he thought.

CHAPTER XXXII

THE DREAM

Although it was still some distance from Trieste, the train was already astir with the projected bustle of its arrival. Passengers were beginning to lock opened suitcases and to pull on their coats and hats. Infected by the unrest, the leisurely Professor left the Misses Flood-Porter and entered his own coupé.

"I don't want to disturb you," he hinted to Iris. "But we shall soon reach Trieste."

Iris showed none of her former morbid reluctance to return to her own carriage.

"I must get my suitcase," she said, eager to impress the Professor with her obedience.

He rewarded her with an approving smile. For the last time she made the shaky journey along the train. Nobody laughed at her or took any notice of her, for every one was too preoccupied with affairs. Suitcases and bags had already been lifted down from racks and stacked outside the carriages, increasing the congestion. Mothers screamed to collect those children who were still chasing each other in the corridors. They washed their chocolate-grimed mouths with corners of moistened handkerchiefs. Banana skins were thrown out of the windows—newspapers bundled under the seats.

The heat and the jam was so oppressive that Iris was actually glad to reach her own compartment. But before she could enter, she shrank back as the doctor came out of the invalid's carriage. His face looked dry and white as the pith of willow above the black blotch of his spade-beard, and his eyes—magnified by his glasses—were dark turgid pools.

As he looked at her, she felt that it was useless to try to deceive him. Like an expert chess player he would have foreseen any possible move of her own and would be prepared with a counter-stroke.

"Is madame better?" he asked.

"Oh, yes. I'm merely slack. Everything seems an effort. And once I sit down I shan't want to move again."

Iris was encouraged by the success of her strategy when the two men exchanged a glance of understanding. She went inside her compartment, but no one appeared to take any interest in her return. The mother and child were reassembling the contents of the family suitcases, while the blonde made an elaborate toilet. The father had taken charge of the Baroness' dressing-bag and was evidently prepared to act as temporary courier.

Iris sat and watched them until the spectacle of noses being powdered and waves reset reminded her of her own need to repair. It was essential to make a good impression at the Embassy. She opened her bag languidly and drew out her flapjack, yawning the while with sudden drowsiness. Blinking her eyes violently, she began to apply powder and lipstick.

But before she could finish, her lids were drooping so continuously that she could not see properly. To her dismay, she realised that she was being overwhelmed with waves of sleep. They were too powerful to resist, although she struggled vainly to keep awake. One after another they swept over her, piling up in a ceaseless procession.

The other passengers began to waver like shadows. Outside, Trieste was visible as a quivering red glow on the night sky. The engine thundered and panted in a last stupendous effort to breast that invisible tape stretched in front of the buffers. Almost abreast, skimmed the vast shadow, with beating wings and swinging scythe.

There was exultation in the stokehold and driver's car, for they were actually ahead of the schedule. Time was beaten, so they relaxed their efforts and slackened speed gradually in readiness for their arrival at Trieste.

Iris' head had fallen forward and her eyes were closed. Then a dog barked in the distance, jerking her awake. As she stared out of the window with clouded gaze, a few scattered lights speckling the darkness told her that they were reaching the outskirts of Trieste.

In that moment she thought of Miss Froy.

"Trieste," she agonised. "I *must* keep awake."

Then, once again, everything grew blurred and she sank back in her corner.

When Hare returned to the carriage his jaw dropped at the sight of her huddled figure. He called to the doctor, who merely rubbed his bony hands with satisfaction.

"Excellent," he said. "She has responded with most extraordinary rapidity."

"But how will I get her out at Trieste?" demanded Hare.

"You will have no trouble. You can wake her at a

245

touch. This is merely preliminary—what you call a cat's-sleep. She will be merely somewhat dazed."

The doctor turned away, but paused to give a word of advice.

"Better leave her alone until you have secured porters. If you wake her too soon she may sleep again. Each time it will be for longer."

Hare took the hint and stood in the corridor, staring out of the window. The reflection of the lighted train flowing over the masonry of roofs and walls transformed them to the semblance of quivering landscape and water. In every carriage luggage was being lowered. Voices shouted for service. The fleeting friendships of a railway journey were being at once sealed and broken in handshakes and farewells.

Iris slept. . . .

In the coupé of the bridal pair, the barrister—Todhunter, for a few minutes longer—was doing his utmost to reconcile a gesture of renunciation with a strategic retreat.

"Shall we say good-bye now?" he suggested. "Before we are surrounded with a cloud of witnesses."

Mrs. Laura ignored his overture.

"Good-bye," she said, carefully curling her lashes upwards. "Thanks for your hospitality. It's been a cheap holiday for me. Cheap in every sense."

In the next coupé the Misses Flood-Porter were facing a major tragedy. It was Miss Flood-Porter who threw the bombshell.

"Rose, did you see the brown suitcase put in the van?"

"No."

"Then I believe it's been left behind. It was pushed under the bed, if you remember."

Their faces were rigid with horror, for their purchases had been packed together for conscientious declaration.

"I was counting on Captain Parker to get them through the Customs for us," lamented Miss Rose. "But it *may* be in the van."

"It may. We can do nothing but hope for the best."

Iris slept on. . . .

When she was a child she suffered from an unsuspected inferiority complex, due to the difference between her lot and that of other children. Although pampered by adults she was exposed to the secret hostility of some of her companions. She was not equal to reprisals, but, at night, her inhibitions found expression in dreams of power, when she sacked the toy-stores and sweet-shops of London with glorious immunity.

Time brought its revenge and Iris got on top of her own little world. But now the Professor's hostility, the antagonism of the doctor and Baroness, together with the derision of the other passengers had combined with her sunstroke to make the old inferiority complex flare up again. The result was that she passed from unconsciousness into one of her childish dreams of power.

She thought she was still on the express and on her way to rescue Miss Froy. The corridors were hundreds of miles long, so that it took her centuries to complete what passed within the limit of a minute. The doctor and a crowd of passengers kept trying to oppose her passage, but she had only to push back their faces, when they dissolved like smoke.

She was mowing them down in swathes when she was aroused by the scream of the engine. Shouts and sudden flashes of light told her that they were rushing into Trieste. Instantly she staggered to her feet—half awake and half in a dream—and walked directly into the next compartment.

Her action took every one by surprise. No one expected it as it was believed that she was asleep. The doctor and the disguised chauffeur were looking out of the window, watching for the arrival of the ambulance. But Hare—who was chatting to the guard—saw her enter, and he made a frantic effort to stop her.

He was too late. Still under the influence of her dream of power and secure in her knowledge of immunity which raised her high above the fear of consequences— Iris rushed towards the invalid and tore the plaster from her face.

The doctor had made the final mistake of an unlucky venture when he gave her the sleeping-draught. Had she carried out her threat to go to the Embassy, she might have encountered incredulity and delay. But the drug had given her the courage to do the impossible thing.

As the criss-cross of strips peeled off and dangled in her fingers like a star-fish, Hare held his breath with horror. Then the guard behind him gave a whistle of astonishment as, instead of spurting blood and raw mutilated flesh, the sound though reddened skin of a middle-aged woman was revealed.

Iris gave a low cry of recognition. "*Miss Froy.*"

CHAPTER XXXIII

THE HERALD

Two days later Iris stood on the platform of Victoria Station, watching the dispersal of the passengers. Among the first to leave were the Misses Flood-Porter. Confident in their right to preferential treatment, they stood aloof with pleased expressions, while an influential gentleman, with an authoritative voice and an infallible method with officials, shouted and shepherded their luggage through the Customs.

Once, by mistake, they looked at Iris, but they were too preoccupied to bow. This was England, where she went out of their lives.

They were very gracious, however, to Mrs. Barnes, when she came to wish them "Good-bye." Her face was radiant with happiness born of a telegram which she had received at Calais.

"Gabriel's cold quite gone very well again."

In spite of her impatience to get home to him she lingered to listen to the last snatch of gossip from the sisters.

"Wasn't it *peculiar* about the honeymoon couple?" asked the elder Miss Flood-Porter. "I know he wasn't on the Venice train, because I looked. And she got off at Milan—alone."

"Yes," nodded Mrs. Barnes. "I know my husband wouldn't like me to say it—but it makes you wonder if they were really married."

"Of course they weren't," scoffed Miss Rose. "I'm precious glad we had nothing to do with them. If there had been a divorce action later on, *we* might have been subpœnaed as witnesses."

"Exactly," agreed her sister. "It just shows how careful one should be when one is abroad. We always keep to our rule *never* to get mixed up in other people's business."

Iris smiled rather bitterly at the conscious virtue in their voices. It reminded her of what she had suffered as a result of their policy of superb isolation. With a shrug she turned her back on the affectionate leave-taking to watch instead the long thin white beams—as of a myriad searchlights—thrown by the sun through the smoky glass roof.

Although she was still shaky she felt quick with fresh life—glad to be back—glad to be alive. While Hare was scouting round the piles of luggage, her thoughts slipped back to the journey. Her memories were dim, with many blanks.

There was a black-out at Trieste, when she crashed completely, and she did not realise her surroundings until she was rushing through the darkness in the Italian train. Some one with lustrous black eyes looked after her, while Hare came and went. She slept most of the time, but whenever she woke she was conscious of happiness.

The carriage was crowded with other passengers, all shouting, smoking and gesticulating. She could not understand a word, but she felt in perfect tune and sympathy with all of them. There was so much happiness in the world with the prospect of joyous reunions. The barriers of language were down, so that they were not alien nationalities but fellow-citizens of the world, united by the common touch.

In the morning she discovered another passenger in the carriage—a little drab, middle-aged woman, with a small lined face and vivid blue eyes.

Iris gave a cry of rapture as she hugged her.

"Miss Froy. You horrible little brute to give me all that trouble. . . . Oh, darling, darling."

In spite of the joy of reunion Miss Froy proved a bad exchange for the Italian stranger. Her fussy attentions, her high tinkling laugh, her incessant chatter, became such a strain that Hare had to scheme for intervals of release.

For all the drawbacks, however, there was a sense of great adventure and high hope about the journey. The wind seemed to blow them along when they travelled across the flat stretches of France. Everything moved with them—streaming smoke and fluttering clouds. The wide fields and white sky swam in light, so that they felt that they were sailing through a magic country.

Although she was better Hare refused to answer any of Iris' questions.

"Tell you in London," he always said.

She reminded him of his promise when he returned with her suitcase, duly chalked.

"I can't wait another minute," she told him.

"Righto," he agreed. "Take a pew."

Squatting together on a luggage truck and smoking cigarettes, she listened to his story.

"It was all very tame. No rough-house—no nothing. The guard was a hero. He knew just what to do, and the doctor and the two nurses went like lambs. You see, they'll probably only be charged with attempted abduction."

"What happened to the Baroness?" asked Iris.

"Oh, she just sailed out, twice her natural size. No connection at all with the next carriage. . . . But she'll pull wires and wangle their discharge. Wheels within wheels, you know."

Iris felt indifferent to their fate.

"What did the others say when they heard about Miss Froy?" she inquired eagerly. "After all, I was right—and every one was out of step but me."

"To be quite candid," said Hare, "it all went in one ear and out at the other. We had a close shave at Venice and some of the Miss Flood-Porters' luggage was missing. They were in such a panic about it that they were prostrate afterwards. And the parson's wife was very worried about her husband."

"But the Professor?"

"Well, he's the sort that doesn't like to be proved wrong. When he saw Miss Froy running about like a two-year-old, he thought it was all exaggerated. I overheard him saying to Miss Flood-Porter, 'People generally get what they invite. I cannot imagine anything of the kind happening to Miss Rose.'"

"Neither can I. . . . Every one seems to be saying good-bye. Here's my Miss Froy."

Hare hurriedly made his escape just in time to avoid

the little woman. She looked wonderfully fit and seemed actually rejuvenated by her terrible experience.

Although she had grown so irritated by the touch of those hard, dry hands, Iris felt a pang of regret now that the parting was near.

"I'm stopping in London for a few hours," confided Miss Froy. "Selfridge's, my dear. Just wandering. Topping."

She looked after Hare as he chased a taxi, and lowered her voice.

"I'm just making up my story to tell them at home. Mater will be *thrilled*."

"But do you think it wise to tell her?" objected Iris. "At her age it might prove a shock."

"Oh, you mean about me." Miss Froy shook her head and gave Iris the conspiratorial wink of one schoolgirl to another. "I'm going to keep mum about *that*. She'd throw a fit and she wouldn't let me go back."

"Are you?" gasped Iris.

"Of course. I shall have to give evidence at the trial, very likely. Besides, all the exciting things seem to happen abroad."

"You're a marvel. . . . But what is the story you're making up?"

Miss Froy grew suddenly young.

"It's about you—and your romance. Is it true?"

Iris did not know herself until that minute.

"Yes," she replied. "I'm going with him on his next trip."

"Then I'm first to congratulate you. And, one day,

perhaps *you'll* congratulate *me*. . . . And now I must fly to send off my wire."

Not long afterwards, a telegram was received at the little grey stone house. Mr. and Mrs. Froy read it together, and later each read it, privately, to Sock.

"Home 8.10 too topping Winnie."

That evening Mrs. Froy stood at the window of Winnie's bedroom. Although she could not see the railway station, she got a glimpse of one amber signal lamp through a gap in the trees.

Everything was ready for her daughter's return. The table was laid in the dining-room and decorated with vases of white dahlias and claret-tinted carrot-tops. The hot-water bottles had been removed from the bed. The rarely-used lamp had been lit in the hall, and the front door thrown open in readiness, so that a strip of light carpeted the mossy garden path.

The supper was keeping hot in the oven. Mrs. Froy always cooked sausages and mashed potatoes for the first meal, under the mistaken impression that it was Winnie's favourite dish. It had been, some thirty years ago—but Winnie never had the heart to undeceive her.

Outside the window was darkness and silence. The stars were frosty and the keen air held the odour of autumnal bonfires. Then, suddenly, the stillness was torn by the scream of the distant train.

Mrs. Froy could trace its approach by the red cloud, quivering above the belt of elms which hid the station. She knew when it stopped, because the engine panted and blew off some steam.

It rattled on again, leaving her guessing. She wondered whether it had brought Winnie. Perhaps she had lost her connection in London. She could see nothing—hear nothing—for she was growing deaf and her eyes were beginning to fail.

The surrounding darkness baffled her and cheated her with unredeemed promises. Figures advanced through the gloom, but—just as her heart leaped in welcome—they always changed back to trees. She strained vainly to catch the first sound of voices—her husband's deep tones and a girl's high-pitched treble.

As she held her breath in suspense, somewhere in the distance a dog barked. Again and again, in frantic excitement. Then through the open gate and up the lighted path charged the clumsy shape of a big shaven dog—capering like an overgrown puppy—whirling round in circles—leaping at his shadow—falling over himself in his blundering haste.

It was the herald who had rushed on ahead, to tell her that the young mistress had come home.

the lady vanishes

Ethel Lina White

savages

Shirley Conran

gone with the wind

Margaret Mitchell

the provincial lady

E. M. Delafield

jaws

☉ ☉ ☉ ❼ ☉ Peter Benchley

the pan book
of horror stories

❼ ☉ ☉ ❼ ☉ Selected by Herbert van Thal

not a penny more,
not a penny less

☉ ☉ ☉ ❼ ☉ Jeffrey Archer

ten stories

☉ ☉ ☉ ❼ ☉ Rudyard Kipling

dead simple

Peter James

last bus to woodstock

Colin Dexter

eye of the needle

Ken Follett

the thirty-nine steps

John Buchan

P A N 7 O

The Hitchhiker's Guide to the Galaxy – Douglas Adams

Born Free – Joy Adamson

Not a Penny More, Not a Penny Less – Jeffrey Archer

Jaws – Peter Benchley

The Dam Busters – Paul Brickhill

The Thirty-Nine Steps – John Buchan

Childhood's End – Arthur C. Clarke

Savages – Shirley Conran

The Provincial Lady – E. M. Delafield

Last Bus to Woodstock – Colin Dexter

The Lost World – Sir Arthur Conan Doyle

Eye of the Needle – Ken Follett

It Shouldn't Happen to a Vet – James Herriot

Dead Simple – Peter James

Ten Stories – Rudyard Kipling

England, Their England – A. G. Macdonell

Gone with the Wind – Margaret Mitchell

The Time Machine – H. G. Wells

The Lady Vanishes – Ethel Lina White

The Pan Book of Horror Stories